Copyright © 2021 by

ISBN: 978-1-387-18971-7

Matt Shaw Publications

All rights reserved. This book or any portion thereof may not be reproduced or used in any manner whatsoever without the express written permission of the publisher except for the use of brief quotations in a book review.

The characters in this book are purely fictitious.

Any likeness to persons living or dead is purely coincidental.

www.facebook.com/mattshawpublications

Signed Books and more
www.mattshawpublications.co.uk

A word from the author:

When I was younger, I used to get a kick out of those *Choose Your Own Adventure* books. Do you remember them? You would read through a chapter (or two) and then, at the end of it, you'd be presented with a "choice" for what your character could do next. If you chose option A, you'd head over to page such and such. If you chose option B, you'd head over to page such and such. Or, if you were me, you would choose an option, flick to the relevant page and have a quick look. If all looked safe, you'd carry on reading. If it didn't, you'd think "fuck that" and automatically choose the *other* option. It was cheating, sure, but some of those game books were hard as balls.

Anyway, I actually released one myself: *A Christmas To Remember*. It was built specifically for Kindle and, it did pretty well but certainly not well enough for me to want to try and repeat the writing process because, no word of a lie, it was a fucking nightmare to do. More so when it came to getting the hyperlinks to work.

This game book is slightly different. For one, it is going straight to hardback and paperback. There will be no electronic version of it and I realise I am narrowing my market but, I just think this particular game will be better with physical copies as opposed to an electric screen. It is also different in that it isn't *your* choice what happens at the end of each segment. Instead, it will be down to a roll of the dice (yes, you'll need a dice to play this game properly). If you don't have a dice, you could use an app to roll a number for you (between 1 and 6) but it's much better with a dice. Well, I say that, I'm sitting here writing this introduction without even writing the book, or testing it, so I could just be talking bollocks, although I do highly doubt it because, you know, I'm great. Cough.

So, to play the game you need a dice. At the end of the section, you give that sexy little cube a roll. When it lands on a number, that dictates where in the book you have to go. Some dice rolls lead to a dead end and other dice rolls lead to various story strands. Play it properly and don't cheat!

I hope you enjoy the book; I probably won't do another one like this given the complicated nature of it but, you know… At least I wrote this one, hey?

**Practise run:**

Roll the dice.

**1** - *close the book*

Give up now and put the book on eBay because it's too much hassle.

**2 - 6** - *continue*

It is fate. You're meant to play this game. So, carry on.

**With thanks to:**

Debbie Alder, Vincent Ashurst, Gareth Baddley, Rachel Barry, Tracy Beattie, Tatjana Billeter, Corinne Bond, James Boyer, John Bradway, Jennifer Brooks, Craig Bullock, Angela Campbell, Wayne Carr, Steve Chappo, Sherry Conroy, Hayley Cooper, Scott Cross, Benjamin Crow, Elson Enciso, Vanessa Fitzpatrick, Mark Flemmich, Sharon Freeman, Catherine Goy, MB Hackney, Sophie Alexandra Hall, Sophie Harris, Steven Heald, Damian Hennessy, Jay Hennigan, Melissa Hitchman, Shaun Hupp, Andrea Kenny, Ann Kerr, Mary Kiefel, Desiree Kilpatrick, Sergey Kochergan, Catherine MacKinnon, Thomas McCormick, Donna Latham, Robyn Leckie, Steve Lowe, Robyn Mattern, Carol McCoy, Rachel Miller, Kirsty Mills, Jessica Mills, Sofie Mondelaers, Patricia Okerns, Leanne Pert, Christina Pfeiffer, Sarah Ponting, Melissa Potter, Kristine Prais, William Rainbow, Emily Randolph, Jill Rogers, Carolanne Rosenberg, Rebecca Ross, Jessica Shelly, Erika L. Shepherd, Kirsty Southern, Victoria Sterling, Crystal Swible, Kerrie Stevens, Tiffany Stewart, Stacey Tewley, Ebony Thurston, Jane Tryner, Lisa Tyrrell, Matthew Vaughn, Ed Williamson-Brown, Katie Elizabeth Weiner, Sharen Womack, Mandy Young

# A ROLL OF THE DICE

AN EXTREME HORROR GAME OF CHANCE

Matt Shaw

# **RULES**

* You need a dice to play this game.
* You must go with the first roll of your dice.
* Re-rolls are only permitted if the dice lands awkwardly and shows two numbers.
* You cannot go back.
* Once you get to the end of the book; the <u>true</u> ending of the story has a note stating it is the proper ending.
* Once you have finished, you can play again to find the other story arcs within the book, but the same rules apply as above.
* Once you've played the game for the first time, if you don't want to play again you can find a story key at the end of the book. This key maps out the majority of the different stories but **does not** highlight them all.
* There are multiple ways to get to various stories so, pray the dice are favourable to you!

# 1

'Is she blind?'

'Maybe she's a retard?'

'Or she thinks he is rich and is only saying "yes" because she thinks he'll buy her lots of presents?'

'It's not your mum, is it?'

Ladies and gentlemen, I present to you, my work colleagues. I wish I could tell you it was all playful banter, but I would be lying. They're just arseholes. We've never seen eye to eye. I've always been the outsider. The office weirdo, just because I am quiet. It's stupid really. I am quiet because they've never tried to be friendly with me. From day one of me being here, a little over a month ago, they've kept me at arm's length, and I have no idea why. That being said, I never tried to give them a reason to like me either. I'm not the sort of person who goes out of my way to make friends with people. Not because I don't want friends, you understand. I'm just shy.

'What if it's his dad?'

'His dad?'

'Yeah. He's going to meet up with him. One of them will be in a wig and a dress.'

'Him or his dad, do you think?'

'Him. I reckon he lets his dad dress him up. Begs him to fuck his "back pussy" hard and deep?'

They laughed.

'Back-pussy? The fuck is a back-pussy?'

'His arsehole.'

'Yeah, I know. I've just never heard it called that before now. That's fucking stupid.'

'Fuck you.'

And now the pack turns on themselves and, amusingly, they do that without me saying a word to them. I never say anything to them. It's not because I am scared of them. It's not because I don't have a witty response for them either. There's just no point in saying anything. It only makes them get louder. They see they're getting to me, they increase their volume. Honestly, they're relentless.

'Is it true?'

Ah, they're back to talking to me again.

'You let your dad fuck your butt?'

'Does he ejaculate in you?'

I said nothing. I just smiled and fondled the dice in my pocket. One day I'll be brave enough to roll it against them. On a roll of one to three, I would do nothing. On a roll of four to six, I'd go home and come back in tomorrow with an assault rifle. I'd tear through the building, unloading clip after clip. Shred their bodies to pieces, pummeling bullets into - and through - them. Splatter their blood and paint the walls with their brains.

'The fuck are you smiling about?'

'Freak.'

Today they're mocking me because I have a date this evening. With the way they talk, they think I am a forty-year-old virgin and that - until tonight - no one had wanted me. They're wrong. I've been married before. A marriage which ended at the roll of a dice.

'How'd you meet? The Internet? Poor bitch probably saw a fake picture you put up, right? She'll take one look at you and storm out.'

'Where are you taking her? McDonalds? Taking her for a Happy Meal?'

'Unhappy meal when she sees what she is stuck with for the night.'

They laughed again.

I do find it amazing how much bullshit they can spout when I'm doing nothing but smiling at them. They just go on and on and on. They're like the *Duracell Bunny*.

What I don't tell them is, my date *is* from the Internet. We met on one of those new dating websites that launched last month, offering a free trial. We've been talking pretty much daily and seem to have a lot in common. Whatever these idiots say, I don't care. I'm looking forward to tonight.

I'm excited about seeing her.

As my work colleagues continued talking shit, I glanced up to the wall clock. It's a little after three. I finish at five. I am meeting my date at seven in a restaurant she picked after I'd given her the choice. Given how she chose it, I presume the food is good. I did have a quick look at the menu, and it seemed to have something of everything and - to my joy -

the prices were reasonable too. That's always a risk you take when you allow your date to choose a place to eat; they could go somewhere with fine dining and high prices to match the supreme quality. The fact she didn't, suggests I might be onto a winner. Who knows, with the right roll of the dice, I could be meeting my next wife tonight.

I smiled at the thought.

If that is the case, I hope it ends better than my first marriage. Guess I'll find out in just a few more hours. Tick. Tock.

# 2

My bedroom mirror's reflection isn't as kind as it could be. The reflection in the shop's mirror had seemed kinder. In the back of my head I keep hearing my work colleagues' taunts about how this woman is going to take one look at me and run. Seeing my reflection, they could well be right.

I'm wearing a black suit. I can't remember who told me, but someone said black was slimming. Looking at my reflection now, I think that person was lying to me. I look fat.

Under the black suit I have a white shirt. I was going to go with a coloured shirt but, instead, went with what I thought was a "classic". Looking at my disappointing reflection now though, I'm worried I might come across as boring. Not only will she think I'm ugly but, she'll think I lack imagination too. A possible fix could be the colour tie that I choose, maybe? I have a number of ties hanging in my closet and not all of them are black, I'm sure.

I walked over to my wardrobe and opened it. The ties were hanging on a small peg, on the back of the right-hand door. There were a number of ties in various shades of black and, amongst them, one pink one which I don't recall buying.

I glanced over to my bed. I had tossed my work clothes there and, with them, my dice. There was a part of me which wondered whether I should roll it to help choose my colour or maybe even, no tie? I could do no tie with a one or two, a black tie on a three or four and the pink tie on the remaining numbers.

My dog, Linds, barked from the corner of the room.

'Yeah, yeah…' I said to her.

I know she was telling me off. *I didn't need to roll a dice for this decision! It was a fucking tie! Surely, I could choose a colour tie without rolling the dice!*

I reached into the wardrobe and pulled out both the pink one, and one of the black ties. I held them both up and turned to Linds.

'How about you decide for me then?'

She cocked her head to the side as though she didn't understand my words. I know she did though. She just didn't want to be responsible for choosing in case my date didn't appreciate it.

Knowing Linds was going to be no use to me, I turned my back on her and looked down at the ties in my hands. Really, it has to be pink. Black would look like I was going to a funeral when put with the rest of my outfit. Pink? Pink showed I was comfortable with my sexuality.

I sighed.

What am I doing?

I looked back at Linds and said, 'I shouldn't go, should I?'

Again, she cocked her head to the side.

'What good are you?' I asked her. Before she could whine, I turned to my dice. 'Okay *this* is a decision for the dice.'

I reached for the dice and grabbed it from the bed. With the question loud and clear in my head - should I go on the date or not - I perched myself on the edge of the bed and rolled the dice onto the top of my bedside cabinet.

## ROLL THE DICE!

**1:** *No hope*
**Go to Chapter 3**

**2 - 3:** *Date Night*
**Go to Chapter 12**

**4 - 6:** *A Quiet Night in*
**Go to Chapter 4**

# 3

I looked at the dice. The dreaded number one stared back at me. It's rare that I set the number by itself, like I had this time. Usually I only do two options: Whatever rolls on one to three or whatever rolls on four to six. Whenever I am low, like today, I set the number one by itself. My way out of this shit-hole once and for all, and it's not just because of the date and the lack of confidence I have going into it. It's everything. It's my whole life is a fucking mess, and I am tired. I am tired of pushing on when it is clear no one really wants me to.

I have money problems, I have dating issues, I have no friends, I live in a shit area, and everything just seems bleak. No, that's not right. It doesn't *seem* bleak. Everything *is* bleak. I'm forty years old and stuck in a dead-end job and it is clear to me now that life is never going to get any better. Here I am looking to go on this date but why? It's not going to work out between us and I'm a fool if I think otherwise. No one will want me - not now and not ever. I was stupid for thinking they would, especially after the end of my first marriage.

Fuck this.

I turned to Linds. She was just sitting there, looking at me with her big brown eyes. Usually, this look was enough to calm my racing thoughts but, not today.

'I'm sorry, girl,' I said. I got up from the edge of the bed and told her, 'You don't need to see this.' Again, she cocked her head. I smiled at her. 'I do love you though.' And, with that, I walked from my bedroom and across the landing to my bathroom.

---

I took my cutthroat razor from my bathroom cabinet. It was tucked behind my medication for depression; pills I was supposed to take but never did as I didn't like how they made me feel.

I opened the blade up and looked at it. It was razor sharp to the touch and would have made a good shaver but, I didn't purchase it for that purpose. If I ever wanted to shave, I had a good electric shaver for that. I bought this because I always figured it would be the best way to kill myself. Quicker than pills for sure.

Linds barked from the doorway. I glanced over. I wasn't even aware that she had followed me. She can probably sense what I am going to do. I smiled at her and said, 'It's okay.'

She barked again.

I got up and walked over to her. There, I dropped to my knees and cuddled her. 'I love you,' I told her, and, with that, I ran the blade of the razor across her throat. She immediately let out a little yelp and tried to get away from my embrace as the blood spurted from her open neck. I cuddled her tighter as her legs gave way and she buckled to the floor. 'It's okay,' I told her. 'I'll see you soon.' I reassured her again, 'I'm right behind you, okay?' As her legs gave way completely, I rolled her onto her side and leaned down to kiss her on the forehead.

Her body stopped twitching.

I was always going to kill her, when I went down this path. There was no way I was going to leave her behind. She had been through the hardest times with me. There was no way I was going to leave her behind. I leaned down and kissed her on the top of her still head again.

Then, I ran the blade across my own throat…

END

**A note from the author:**

**Yeah, okay, this was bleak and really short. The reason for this particular chapter was not because I take pleasure in killing animals in my books but because I wanted to show you how quickly you can ruin your own life by playing games of chance. A quick little life lesson for you before you play the game properly. Anyway, go back to the end of Chapter 2 and roll the dice again. If you're unlucky to get a 1 again, just re-roll so you're not just stuck in a loop reading this chapter. Be warned though; this is the only time you will be allowed to go back to the previous chapter for a "redo". Moving forward, there is to be no cheating.**

# 4

The dice had spoken. I would have a quiet night in instead. Once again, the Gods of the dice smile down upon me for, the more I think about it, the more I think that is the best decision. She'd only be disappointed when she saw me. Worse yet? I'd probably look at her and fall head over heels in love with her. I do that a lot and - almost always - it is never really reciprocated.

Linds whined from the corner of the room. I looked away from the dice and over to her. 'You think I'm making a mistake?' I asked.

'No,' she said. It wasn't the first time she had spoken to me, not that she ever talked in front of other people. It was only when we were alone.

'Good because I can't go against the dice. You know that.' That was my rule. Never go against what the dice tell me to do.

'I know,' she said.

She walked over to me and sat next to me. I smiled at her and slid myself off the bed and onto the floor. The moment I did so, she nuzzled into me and I put my arm around her.

'I didn't want you to go anyway,' she said.

'So why didn't you say something?'

'Because you seemed excited about it.'

For a time I had been, I guess. It had been a while since I'd gone on a date. But then, my confidence levels changed daily so I wasn't surprised I had got cold feet when it actually came down to it. Now I was grateful for how the dice rolled as it saved me having to go and, as a result of going, getting sick in my stomach with nerves.

I said to Linds, 'But if you didn't want me to go, I wouldn't have. You know I don't want to upset you.' I rubbed her hairy chest and told her, 'You're my special little girl.'

In response to my touch, her tail wagged enthusiastically and she stood up until we were face to face. She immediately started licking my face with her warm, wet tongue. I laughed and tickled the sides of her face as she did so. The more I laughed and tickled her, the more her tail wagged from side to side.

She stopped a moment and told me, 'And you know I love you too.'

I smiled.

It was always nice to hear that she loved me. I don't care how cold a person is, if a dog tells you they love you, it makes you feel good. She licked my mouth. In response, I opened my mouth and poked my tongue out flat. With a wagging tail, she started licking it as I felt my cock start to harden.

Between her licks, she asked, 'Can I make you happy?'

Not wanting to force myself on her, I told her, 'You don't have to, if you don't want to.'

'I wouldn't offer if I didn't want to,' she said as she buried her face into my crotch. I flinched away and pushed her back a moment. 'What's wrong?' she asked.

'Nothing,' I said. I fumbled with my leather belt and undid it. She watched, with a cocked head, as I reached for the bedside drawer. She knew what was coming and - in anticipation - she licked her lips in the same way she did whenever I was serving up her dinner.

'What flavour?' I asked.

I pulled two bottles of lubricant out of the drawer. One was flavoured mint and the other; strawberry.

'Do you have chocolate?' she asked.

'You ate that one last time,' I said.

I could see the disappointment on her face. In fairness, I had meant to order another tube but it had slipped my mind. 'How about strawberry?' I asked.

She barked.

I squirted a healthy load of flavoured gel into the palm of my hand. Unable to wait, Linds immediately started to sniff it. She even gave it a test lick before I pulled my hand away and told her, 'Wait.'

She sat on her bum and patiently waited, and watched, as I reached down into my trousers, and shorts, to my cock and - with a gel-free hand - I pulled it out. It stood tall and proud as I started to rub the lube all over my shaft, helmet and balls.

'Wait…' I told her.

She licked her lips again. I could see she was dying to get a taste and, given how she was doing me the favour, I didn't want to keep her waiting. I pulled myself up on the bed and perched on the edge of the mattress with my legs apart.

'Okay!' I told her; her cue to know that she was allowed to get to licking up the lube. Immediately she jumped up and buried her head in my crotch. 'Oh fuck,' I sighed as her tongue started lapping up against my bollocks. 'You know the spot, don't you?' Her tail wagged from side to side as she concentrated on licking me clean. Warm spit wetted up my shaft and I couldn't stop myself from sighing again as, between her licks, I started to stroke myself up and down, up and down... 'You're a good girl,' I said as she continued to lick enthusiastically.

She paused a moment and said, 'More... I want more...'

So as not to ruin the flow, I quickly grabbed the tube of lube and squirted it down over my throbbing prick. In turn, Linds went straight back to licking it up.

'You keep up with that,' I warned her, 'and I'm going to fucking cum.'

She momentarily pulled away and replied, 'Good. I want you to shoot it into my mouth. Let me taste you.'

That was it. She knew I loved it when she talked dirty. My legs tingled first. A split second, my testicles did the same and - then - my body jolted as I shot a thick load of cum over her face, some of which she expertly caught in her hungry mouth.

As she swallowed it down, she barked.

I just sat there a moment and caught my breath. Whenever I was with her, the orgasms were always intense and would take me a couple of minutes to calm down. Basking in the pleasure given, I laughed. 'Man's best friend,' I told her as I gave her another nuzzle.

# 5

The warm shower water cascaded over me and washed the shitty day clean away. I was standing there with my head down, watching the dirty water swirl away down the plughole.

I had to keep myself steady with a strong hand on the tiled wall. As always, the orgasm had taken it right out of me - not that I was complaining. Before Linds had helped alleviate my stress, I had been getting myself worked up with the shitty day that I'd had but, as always, she had managed to calm me right down and make me realise I was just being stupid.

The problem was, I was so calm now, I wasn't sure whether I wanted to go on the date after all. If I was quick out of the shower, I would have been able to get there still. I'd just be a little late but, a text would sort that. A little warning that I was stuck in traffic, or something. A little reassurance that I was still coming, and I would make it up to her by allowing her three courses from the menu.

No.

I can't say that.

I don't care if she wanted three courses. If I put that in a text, she might think I am being serious and think of me as tight-arse. Not a good first impression to make.

I turned the taps off. The flow of water pouring over me turned to a drip. I stepped out of the shower and grabbed a towel from the side. As I did so, I caught sight of myself, naked, in the bathroom mirror.

I smiled.

This mirror is kinder in here and, in this light, I can't help but think I could have made a good first impression on my date. Fuck. Maybe I should have gone. Maybe I've let the dice steer me away from a real happy ending and not a "temporary" happy ending, as provided by Linds. Perhaps, under the circumstances, I can do a re-roll? Go on the date after all or get an early night? It's not cheating because there is a different option thrown in.

Linds barked and I jumped.

She was standing in the doorway, watching me. I hadn't realised.

'How long have you been standing there?'

She turned away and went back into the bedroom. I wrapped the towel around me and followed. She jumped up onto the bed and laid down. She didn't need to say anything. I knew what she wanted. She wanted me to go in and cuddle up with her.

I couldn't just do that though. Not without giving the dice a roll. You know - just to be sure fate wanted me to stay home.

**ROLL THE DICE!**

**1-5:** *Date Night*
**Go to Chapter 12**

**6:** *Tomorrow is another day*
**Go to Chapter 6**

# 6

Fuck it. Who am I trying to kid? I always do this. I get my hopes up about something only to find my hopes were very much misplaced. This is why I do a roll of the dice; it saves me making a mistake and fucking things up for myself.

I won't go on the date. She might be pissed at me for standing her up but, really, she'll find someone else to go out with pretty fast. What's more, they'll be a better fit with her than me. Anyway, look at Linds…

Linds rolled onto her back and showed her belly. This was the norm; she would pleasure me and then she would expect belly rubs for a job well done. It wouldn't be fair for me to just leave her. Not without giving her the deserved rubs.

With the towel around my waist still, I walked over to the bed and made myself comfortable on it, next to Linds.

'Are you going to give me some belly rubs?' she asked.

I smiled at her. 'You know I am.'

'I wasn't sure for a moment. I thought you might go on the date still.'

I shook my head. 'I wouldn't do that to you,' I told her as I started to tickle her belly. She stretched out so I could get every inch of her belly. I like my dick licked, she likes this. We all have our pleasures. 'That nice, girl?'

She said nothing. She just laid there, stretched out and panting with excitement. I smiled. There was no way I could go on the date and not give her this moment. No way on earth and, thankfully, the dice knew that.

'You're a good girl,' I told her.

# 7

I woke up with a start. I was still on the bed wrapped in the towel. Linds was on the other side of the bed, stretched out and snoring on her side. I must have been more tired than I thought and dozed off whilst I was stroking her belly. Hopefully I had given her enough tickles to make her feel satisfied. The last thing I want to do is short-change her from belly-rubs after she'd made me cum so hard.

I sat up and looked back at her. She didn't stir at all, which suggested she was more than satisfied with how the night ended. Otherwise, she would have been staring at me already and, more to the point, on her back again and showing off her belly.

I reached over to my phone and looked at the time. It was a little after seven in the morning. I was surprised I had managed to sleep right through but, I must have needed it. On my phone, I also noticed eight missed calls and a little envelope showing I had a waiting text message. The calls were all from the same number and I was surprised to see her name there. She must have got to the restaurant and just sat and waited for me. Weirdly I don't feel guilty about standing her up. Especially when I had already decided I was doing her a favour but not showing up. Still, curious, I opened up the waiting message. I couldn't help but smile when I read it. It simply read: *You're an asshole.* And that would be the impression she'd got from me even if I had shown up so, again, I saved us both some time.

I climbed from my bed and walked through to the ensuite bathroom where I let the towel drop to the tiled floor. I took an early morning piss and then looked at my reflection to see what kind of state I was in today. My dark hair was all over the place, I had bags under my eyes and my eyes themselves were a bright pink in colour. My skin was pale too and I'm sure that wasn't down to the light. I actually looked as though I were coming down with something. I didn't feel too bad but, maybe I did have a bug?

From the bedroom, my alarm rang out on my phone. I sighed as Linds barked for it to, 'Shut the fuck up.' She was always a grumpy bitch whenever she was woken in the morning, so I hurried through to the bedroom and killed the alarm.

'You're okay,' I told her. 'Go back to sleep for a bit, if you want, whilst I get ready for work.' She didn't need the invitation. She was already laying back on her side with her eyes closed. Oh, to be a dog. To get to stay at home all day and just sleep away the hours or sit and chew on a favourite toy. The life of Riley, right there. I caught sight of myself in the bedroom mirror. Just as I had done so yesterday, I looked worse in this mirror and I couldn't help but feel a pang of jealousy when I thought about Linds' life.

'What do you think?' I asked, 'Should I stay home with you today? We could just laze around all day and watch television.' It was wishful thinking: I'd already had too many days off work. Anymore and I was at risk of losing my quarterly bonus. I'd have to go to work. The only question was: Do I go to work with a smile on my face or do I go to work with a gun in hand?

I looked back at my depressing reflection. I've often thought about going to work with a gun and shooting those assholes down. Maybe today is the day I should do just that? My reflection is nodding at me. *He* seems to think it is a good idea. Luckily it isn't just up to *him* though. We all know his judgement isn't the soundest. It's up to the dice.

**ROLL THE DICE!**

**1-2 -** *Keep on Smiling!*
**Go to Chapter 8**

**3-6 -** *BANG!*
**Go to Chapter 9**

# 8

I smiled as I walked into the office, just as I did every other day even though they never smiled back at me. No sooner had I taken my seat did the jibes start.

'So? How was seeing your dad last night?'

'Did he look mighty pretty in his dress?'

'That was his dad? Fuck. I saw them out and about, heading for McDonalds, and I honestly thought that hairy chinned cunt was his mum!'

They laughed. I said nothing as I fired up my computer, ready to start my day of inputting figures. That was all I did. I took figures from one spread sheet and put them in another, day in and day out. It was a boring job and I hated it but, I couldn't complain too much as it paid the bills and even left a little spare in my pocket each month.

'You fucked, didn't you? I can smell it on you. You stink like dry spunk in a sponge.'

'Shit is that smell him? I thought the drains had gone.'

'No, it's him. I smelled it the moment he walked in.'

'Fucking rancid.'

'Yeah, but I still want to know if he got his mum pregnant last night. A box of McChicken Nuggets, a quick finger blast and then dolloped his premature ejaculate into her by hand. Spoon-fed that bitch.'

I just kept on smiling. When they laughed, I laughed. As always, I wanted to tell them to fuck off, or to go and fuck themselves. I even wanted to insult their families... One of them had just had a baby with their wife. A perfect insult to that prick being, *I saw pictures of your baby. Did you order it from WISH?* The joke being that whenever you ordered something from that website, it always came through looking kind of retarded. As always though I said nothing. If I was supposed to punish them for how they spoke to me then the dice would have allowed it. Clearly, the way the dice protected them, there are bigger plans for them. I'm not sure what they are but, it's not my place to question the dice. I just do as it says.

'Seriously, mate,' one of the asked, 'did she even show up? Or were you left Billy-No-Mates in the restaurant?'

'Oh fuck, that's embarrassing. How long did you wait?'

'Did the waiters feel sorry for you? Did they get you a drink and meal on the house to try and make you feel better. Oh shit… Please don't tell us you cried into your tomato soup…'

They laughed. I laughed. Oh, they're so funny.

'No one is ever going to want you. You know that, right? No one is ever going to want you and you're going to die poor and alone.'

'He's right. You're fucking hopeless.'

The thing is, they were probably right.

'You know what you should do? You should probably kill yourself.'

'Whoa, Jack, don't say that…'

'No?'

'No. He should *definitely* kill himself.'

They laughed. I laughed.

And then I said, 'You're right.'

'What?'

I stood up from behind my desk. I told them again, 'You're right.'

None of them were laughing. Despite the smile on my face, a tear rolled down my cheek.

'We're just joking, mate.'

'Yeah, we're just teasing.'

'No. No. You're absolutely right. I should have done it long ago.'

'Come on, we're just playing around.'

Before they could say anything else, I stepped from behind my desk and ran - full pelt - towards the large window at the far end of the office. They watched in horror as, when near to the window, I grabbed a chair and tossed it ahead of me.

The chair flew through the air and smashed through the window before I got to it. When I was nearer, I jumped - still with a smile on my face… That was what the dice wanted; it wanted me to go to work with a smile on my face. I had done that. It didn't tell me what to do once I had got there.

I crashed through the window - still with a smile - and plummeted the ten stories down towards the car park below.

A few feet away from my concrete death, the world turned black and everything shut down.

**END**

**A note from the author:**

Either play again or go to the back of the book for a guide to which chapters run together, to give you another reading experience. Obviously, I suggest you play again but, each to their own!

# 9

I smiled as I parked my car up in my usual parking spot at the office. When I first woke up, I really wasn't sure how the day was going to go but - evidently - the dice were really looking out for me today.

I killed the engine and my grin widened as I realised the car's old engine wouldn't be the only thing I was killing today.

With a spring in my step, I threw the car door open and jumped from the vehicle. I closed the door behind me and went round to the trunk. At the press of a button, the trunk popped open, revealing my sports bag. With effort, I pulled the heavy bag out and slammed the trunk shut again. Given how my day was going to be going, I didn't bother locking the car and - instead - I headed towards the office block. With each step, I hummed *Hey-Ho, Hey-Ho, it's off to work we go*.... I don't know why and, by the time I pushed the office door open, I had already annoyed myself.

Still, I won't let anything ruin my day. These cunts have had this coming for a long, long time.

As the office door closed behind me, the building's security guard looked up. He didn't bother to smile. He recognised me as a worker and went back to the newspaper he was trying, unsuccessfully, to keep hidden behind his desk.

I walked up to the elevator, set my bag down and pressed the call button. I then watched impatiently as the various floors illuminated on the panel, above the lift's closed doors, showing where the elevator was.

'Come on, come on,' I muttered to myself.

Finally, the doors opened and I grabbed my bag and stepped in. I pressed the button for my floor, several stories up, and the doors closed - thankfully before anyone else got in here as it gave me time to prepare.

As the lift started its journey upwards, I set the bag down on the floor and unzipped the bag's heavy-duty zipper. I pulled the bag open and smiled at the sight of the various weapons I had so merrily packed this morning; kitchen knives, a cleaver, a hand axe and a handgun I'd purchased from the blackmarket when people kept trying to break into my home. Funny really, I never expected I would actually be using the gun when I bought it. I was just going to catch the fuckers in the act of trying to break in and - from there - I was going to wave it in their faces. The plan being that it would be enough to scare them away once and for all. Typically, once I bought the gun, they stopped trying to break in. Still, I had no regrets about spending all the money on buying it. It was nice to feel safe in my house and - of course - it was even nicer now.

I took the gun out and set it to the side before I started hiding the various blades around my body. The axe I tucked between shirt and trousers; it was a little harder to hide this one but, it didn't matter. I didn't exactly plan to hang around once the elevator doors opened and speaking of which…

I stood just in time for the lift doors to ping open. Gun in hand, already loaded and primed, I was ready. I've dreamed of this moment for so long, despite the fact I'd only rolled for it for the first time today. I just hoped it could live up to the high expectations I had set in my mind.

With a twisted grin on my face, I stepped out into the open plan office and shouted, 'Morning, fuckers!'

# 10

I raised the gun towards the cunt behind the first desk. His confused face turned to one of fear in the blink of an eye. As I raised the gun's primed barrel up, he raised his hands to his face as though that were going to protect him. I winked at him as I squeezed the sensitive trigger.

The gun kicked back as a bullet exploded from the barrel. Faster than could be seen, it flew through both the air and his hand before it lodged deep in his head. The force of the shot kicked his head back and toppled him from his chair as, around me, the room erupted into screams of terror.

I felt as though I was Beethoven, and this was my orchestra. Sing for me, you fuckers.

I turned, gun still raised, and pointed at another "colleague" as they ran for the fire escape. I pulled the trigger for a second time and stuck a bullet into their spinal column. They fell forward and sprawled out on the carpeted tiles. I'm not sure if they're dead but I know they won't walk again if they do survive.

I span and fired again.

A woman's brains splattered white and red up the wall she was cowering near. Her body slumped to the side as her friend screamed next to her. Her scream was cut short with a bullet to the chest, and she too fell to the side as she wheezed, desperate for air.

'Fuck you!' I screamed at them all.

I turned and fired again and again and again…

More bodies on the floor. Blood splattered up the walls and over the office furniture as I laughed for what felt like the first time in as long as I could remember. Fuck these cunts. Each and every one of them deserved it.

'Please… Don't…' Words cut off as a bullet penetrated the obnoxious fuck's mouth, shattering the front teeth in the process before obliterating the back of his head and splashing skull and gore over a metal filing cabinet.

Next.

A bullet through the eye and out the back of the head.

Next.

A bullet to the groin and a change of pitch to the screaming.

Next.

A bullet through the neck and a jettison of claret which shot at least a foot away from where they staggered, up until they collapsed to the floor with a panicked hand pressed to the wound. They wouldn't survive.

Next.

I squeezed the trigger and the gun clicked.

'FUCK!' I yelled. When I had purchased the gun from the council estate, I only bought one round of ammo as I didn't think I would be needing more. I regret that decision.

I dropped the empty gun on the floor and screamed.

I turned around in time to see my old manager (I presume I've been fired) racing towards me with a look of hate in his eyes. Quickly, I pulled the hand-axe out and swung it. The fucker ran directly into the sharpened blade. It wedged directly between his eyes, splitting his nose near enough in two as well. A cracking shot and, for a moment, we both stood there stuck in a dance; him on his feet being pulled around by me controlling him by yanking on the axe's wooden handle. Fucking thing was stuck in him, much to my disappointment.

I couldn't stop to worry about it and released my grip. Both manager and axe fell to the floor as one. Not done yet, despite the distant sirens nearing the office block, I pulled out a kitchen knife and stalked towards where I could see another woman (whore) hiding.

In this office, no one is innocent.

# 11

I reached over the desk and grabbed the slag by her hair. I yanked her up to her feet as she screamed in terror. Silly bitch. Had she really thought I couldn't see her down there?

'Please don't,' she said, 'I have a daughter.'

Curious, I asked, 'Do you know who the father is?'

Before she could answer I ran the knife across her throat, opening a wide gash in the process. A gash which spat warm blood over me which, I won't lie, took me by surprise. I pushed her back and she landed in what used to be her office chair. She raised her hands to her neck and tried to stop the blood but, we both knew it was too late for her. She would be dead in less than a minute.

I didn't bother to wipe the blade clean as I span on my heels to see who else I could spot, hiding.

The sirens were really loud now. The police were downstairs and I knew it wouldn't be long before they would be storming the building. I guess there was only one thing left to do now: Roll the dice and see how this game ended. On a roll of one to three, I surrender and let them have their justice. On a roll of four to six, I try and send as many of them to Hell as I can before they put a bullet in me and stop this wild ride.

With my spare hand, I reached into my pocket for my dice. My heart skipped a beat when I realised it wasn't in there. Quickly, I checked the other pocket and - still - there was nothing.

'Shit,' I mumbled. In my haste to load up the bag of weapons, I had left the dice on the table where I'd last rolled it.

Deflated, I sat down on the edge of one of the desks. It creaked underweight but I knew it would hold me.

I don't know what to do now.

I can't recall the last time I had made a true choice for myself and - my world started to spin. A second later and I retched heavily before I threw up an acidic puddle of stomach bile yakked straight up from the depths of my rippling gut. Traces remained in my throat, burning away as - across the open plan office - the elevator doors opened, and armed police came filing out with guns raised.

I screamed at them, 'I don't know what to do!'

**END**

**A note from the author:**

**Either play again or go to the back of the book for a guide to which chapters run together, to give you another reading experience. Obviously, I suggest you play again but, each to their own!**

# 12

'I'm sorry I'm late,' I told her as I took a seat opposite her.

She smiled at me and confessed, 'I wasn't sure if you were going to show up.'

'Traffic was a nightmare,' I told her.

'You're here now,' she said. She almost sounded relieved.

'I hope you haven't been waiting too long.'

She laughed.

'Uh oh,' I said. 'I take that as a *you've been waiting for a while*.'

'It's my own fault. I've one of those annoying people who get to places early. You know, just in case traffic is bad or something.'

'I guess I should learn from you,' I said.

'No, not at all. It's just how I prefer to do things.'

'So how long have you been waiting?'

She laughed again. 'Long enough for two glasses of wine.'

Surprised, I looked at the glass of white she was cradling in her hands. 'That's your second or third?'

She smiled. 'I mean I'm not an alcoholic but, this is my third now.'

'Damn. I guess I have some catching up to do? Should I just order myself a stack of shots?'

On cue, the waiter approached the table and asked, 'Good evening. Can I get you anything to drink?'

'Sure,' I said. 'I'll have the same as the lady.'

'Certainly, sir.'

I didn't offer her another drink seeing as she'd barely touched this one. As the waiter walked away, I panicked as to whether I still should have asked her if she wanted anything. Maybe she was bored with wine and wanted some water? 'Shit, did you need anything else?'

'I'm fine,' she said.

I noticed her menu was on the edge of the table, close to her glass. Unlike the menu on my side of the table, hers was closed over.

'I take it you've been here long enough to know what you want to eat?'

She laughed. 'I don't know if I should admit to this…'

Curious I asked, 'What?'

'I chose at home.'

'You chose at home?'

'On their website. I looked at the menu and pre-chose what I wanted.'

'You did?'

'I'm terrible when it comes to choosing something to eat,' she said. With the way she spoke, she almost seemed embarrassed by what she was saying. 'People are usually waiting for me to decide.'

'Well, I mean, you waited for me to show up so it would have only been fair for me to wait for you to choose something to eat, right?'

She laughed again. However, this night ends, at least I've been able to make her laugh a few times. Given how long it has been since I've been on a date, I'd still call it a success.

'Anyway, that's not embarrassing,' I told her.

'It's not?'

'Forward planning. Saves time. It's sensible. You want to know what is embarrassing?'

'What?'

I reached into my pocket and put the dice down on the table.

'What's that for?' she asked.

Normally I don't pull the dice out so early but, if we were to see each other again then she needed to know about my habits now. That way I wouldn't waste either of our time if she found it weird and wanted to leave me over it. Although if that did happen, I would be disappointed.

'Decisions.'

'It's for decisions?'

'I live my life through chance,' I told her. Whenever a series of decisions come up, I roll a dice to help me choose. You'll see me roll it when it comes to choosing what to eat too, unless there is something I simply can't live without on the menu. If there's more than one option that I'd eat, I roll the dice.'

From the look on her face, I could tell she didn't know whether to believe me or not. 'Really?' she asked. I nodded. She laughed and said, 'Yeah that is weirder than choosing what to eat using the restaurant's website.'

I laughed too. 'See, I told you your way of ordering wasn't weird.'

'So do you have any other weird habits or hobbies?'

I smiled at her. 'Well, we can't give away all of our secrets on a first date, can we?'

She blushed and then, weirdly, so did I. Perhaps I had been too presumptuous but - from this short time together, I was hoping for a second date. Maybe she was hoping for an evening to just fly by so she could get out of here and away from me?

I quickly added, 'Need something to talk about if you want a second date by the end of the evening.' Then, to save digging myself a hole, I asked, 'So what do you recommend here?' I broke eye contact and grabbed the menu.

# 13

'How did it feel?' she asked as I finished my dessert off; a tasty creme brûlée. She was referring to the fact I hadn't used my dice at all throughout our meal together. I had wanted to, but she clearly wanted to test me as she'd asked if she could choose for me. I knew I liked her, so I decided to give her the benefit of the doubt, although I didn't just let her choose from the whole menu. Instead, I went through and picked a few options out and then, from those options, she chose my starter, my main and my dessert.

'It felt…' I paused a moment as I mulled over how it actually *did* feel. Then, I said, 'Fine. It felt fine.'

'Well, I guess "fine" is better than horrible,' she said.

'Fine is definitely better than horrible.' I set my spoon down after resisting the urge to lick it clean in front of her.

Throughout the meal, we had talked about this and that. She had told me what she did for a living (a teacher) and I had told her what I did for a living (data inputting for a major firm). Her job definitely sounded more interesting, but also harder as she explained some of the kids (well, teenagers) came from rather "interesting" backgrounds and had clearly picked up bad habits which were hard to deal with sometimes. I didn't envy her.

One thing I noticed, above all else throughout the meal, was that there was a lot of laughter too. She said things which made me chuckle and I said things which made her laugh too. It was nice and a far cry from conversations I'd have with people at work, or even back when I actually used to have friends. "Used" to have friends because, really, they were never really mine in the first place. It was more like they tolerated me because they were friends with my wife. When she left, they did too.

We hadn't discussed my ex and neither had we discussed any ex-partners she might have had. I realise we all have a past but, I don't need to hear about other guys she used to see. I find it all rather hard to swallow as my imagination starts picturing her with them and I find myself questioning whether she laughed as much with them, or more. It's not a healthy way to be.

As we waited for the waiter to come and clear away our desserts, I knew I didn't want the evening to end. A quick check on the time and it wasn't too late to offer an extended evening with a drink someplace else. I shifted nervously in my seat as I prepared myself mentally to ask the question.

She frowned. 'What's wrong?'

'Is it that obvious something's on my mind?'

She nodded. 'Pretty much.'

I laughed, mostly out of embarrassment.

'Well,' I said hesitantly, 'I was just wondering if you wanted to go someplace else and get another drink?'

She smiled. I took that as a good sign. 'I'm not sure,' she said.

'I mean we don't have to. I just didn't want the evening to end yet,' I admitted.

She leaned across the table and took the dice from where I'd left it next to me. She raised it to her face and said, 'If I roll a one to three, I'll go back to yours for a coffee… If I roll a four to six, I'll go home and get an early night ahead of a busy day at work tomorrow,' she said.

I felt a pang of excitement at the sight of her using the dice to decide her future. Or was the pang of excitement due to the fact I knew "coffee" didn't just mean a hot drink?

My heart skipped a beat as she blew on the dice and then shook it in her hand before letting it roll onto the table.

The dice tumbled across the surface, towards where I was sitting.

**ROLL THE DICE!**

**1-4 -** *The date continues*
**Go to Chapter 19**

**5-6 -** *She goes home alone*
**Go to Chapter 14**

# 14

After watching her leave, I pulled out of the carpark frustrated - both mentally and sexually. When she rolled a five, I was genuinely disappointed. From her face, I thought she was too, and, for a moment, I actually believed she might have rolled it again until she got the number she wanted. She didn't. I even asked her, 'You're not going to re-roll?' She asked if I did that and, I couldn't lie. I said, 'no.' Then she wouldn't either. I asked her if I would see her again and she looked down to the dice. She said that it might be an idea for me to roll it as clearly the dice and her were not friends.

I couldn't roll it. I wanted to see her again and wasn't sure how I would react if the dice said that wasn't an option.

She asked where that left us and - stupidly - I said it left us in stalemate.

When she left, she wasn't happy. She didn't understand why I needed a dice to say if I wanted to see her again. I told her I didn't but, because of how I live my life it was what I needed to do. She didn't get it and said I was welcome to call her when I was ready to stop playing games.

I don't know… Watching her get her coat and walk out of the restaurant hurt. It was like a knife to the chest, straight through the heart but I couldn't run after her because I couldn't just go against what I believed in and invite her for a second date without a roll of the dice and, well, they'd already fucked me over once this night and that was bad enough. What if I rolled and they said I couldn't see her again?

As I drove down the narrow streets, away from the restaurant, I didn't know where I was going. I just knew I didn't want to go home as there was nothing there for me but bed. Sitting with her all night had felt great and made me realise just how much I missed human companionship; something I had never thought I would be found thinking and yet here I was, thinking just that. Now I was wondering how much my depression was fed through loneliness alone.

I stopped at the traffic lights as they turned red. Turning right would take me home. Turning left would extend my evening. I didn't want to go home but I knew, by my own rules, I couldn't just turn left. So, what was it to be then? With the lights not changing any time soon, I reached into my pocket and took the dice out. So, come on then, what is it to be? Do I go home, go to bed and start a new day tomorrow or do I live a little and have some fun?

On a roll of one to three, I turn left.

Four to fix and I turn right.

I tossed the dice onto the seat next to me and watched as it bounced off and down into the footwell out of sight.

The red light ahead of me turned amber and then green.

Fuck it, I'm sure it's telling me to turn left and to live a little. I flicked my indicator and took a left-hand turn towards the industrial estate. It wasn't the first time I had taken a drive down there, long after most of the warehouses shut up shop for the night, although - it had been a while since I'd last visited. That being said, last time I drove down it was about eight o'clock and there had been a good selection to choose from. It's gone half ten now and there is a part of me which worried whether I'd just be left with the dregs to choose from.

Oh well. What was the saying again? *Any port in a storm.*

# 15

Ahead of me, gathered under a flickering streetlamp, there was a group of prostitutes. They were standing around chatting amongst themselves. Even from this distance, with how little they were wearing, I could see some of them shivering in the cold night's air. Someone had lit a small fire in a metal trash can nearby but clearly the flames weren't offering enough heat. Unless they were shivering from withdrawals. I know from experience that some of the ladies down here like to inject so, it wouldn't surprise me. Not only had I seen the tell-tale marks on their arms, when I was fucking them, but I had also seen discarded needles littered on the dirty ground of the alleyway we'd conducted our business in. Each to their own, it wasn't as though I ever barebacked them, so I was pretty safe from whatever shit was in their blood.

I sat there for a moment, parked up on the side of one the small roads which snaked around the estate. From this distance I couldn't really see their faces properly but that didn't bother me too much. Whenever I came here, we tended to go up the alley to fuck. They would put their hands on the wall, with their arse facing me. I would stick it in from behind and that's the position we would stay in, right up until I shot my load into the rubber. Sometimes I'd be in their cunt. Sometimes, for as little as an extra tenner, I'd be tearing them a new arsehole. Whatever the hole, in that position you didn't tend to see their face, so it really didn't matter what they looked like. All I cared about was their body. I liked the thin women and, with most of them addicted to crack (at least) here, all the whores I could see over there had bodies which met my preference.

The only thing that was bothering me was the fact that I had cheated myself to be here. I hadn't seen the actual number on the dice and, well, that went against everything I believed in. I knew I couldn't just leave it either because if I was really willing to cheat like that, I could have been at home with my dating continuing. If I was going to cheat,

I'd much sooner cheat to get something more worthwhile like that, and not just a quick fuck with some cheap skank.

'I can't do it,' I mumbled. I leaned over to the passenger side of the car and fumbled around blindly on the floor, looking for the dice. When I found it, I carefully pulled it out to see the number it had rested on. To my delight, it had ended up on a two and so, I was where I was supposed to be.

*What if it rolled over when you turned the corner?* A little voice challenged me in the forefront of my mind. *The only way you can be sure is if you roll it again.* It wasn't the first time I'd heard such a voice in my head, and I knew I couldn't ignore it, just as I couldn't ignore the rolling of the dice.

'Fine,' I mumbled. 'So what now?'

*You need to re-roll. Just to be sure.*

I wasn't happy but I knew the voice was right. If I wanted to be sure I was doing the right thing, I would have to roll the dice again. This wasn't cheating. Whenever you weren't entirely sure of the result, you were allowed to roll again. This usually happened when the dice landed on an edge though, propped up against something so that it showed two numbers. It didn't happen often, but it *did* happen occasionally.

Right. Fine.

If I roll a one to three, I stay.

If I roll above, I go home and I go to bed and then - tomorrow - I go to work with a smile on my face just as I always do.

I closed my hand around the dice and gave it a shake.

**ROLL THE DICE!**

**1-3:** *Whore!*
**Go to Chapter 16**

**4-6:** *Tomorrow's another day*
**Go to Chapter 8**

# 16

The dice had spoken and I felt a twinge of anticipation from between my legs. I flashed my headlights to get the women's attention and - sure enough - they all turned and peered in my direction. Just as I couldn't really make out their faces, they couldn't really see mine either but, with habits to support, they weren't bothered about appearances either.

One lady headed over to where I was parked. I tried not to laugh as she did her best to walk "sexy"; swaying her hips, one hand on her hip and one hand played with her long, brown hair. God loves a trier.

In preparation for our conversation, I put the driver's window down and gave a quick check of how much cash I had in my wallet. Three tens and a single twenty. With these ladies, that would afford me the top of their menu and I could probably get it cheaper still, if I tried. On any other day I would have too but, today, I just wanted to cum and be done. Chatting shit and haggling prices only delayed my own gratification.

'Hey, baby,' she said as she leaned down to the window. The sink of cigarettes hanging heavy on her breath also made me gag on the spot but, thankfully, I managed to contain it. It didn't matter if she stunk of rotten meat and yesterday's dick cheese once the conversation was over with. I'd still be fucking her from behind so it wouldn't be in my face like it would have been if missionary was my pleasure. 'Were you looking to party?'

I smiled. Up close she really is rancid to look at but, so long as down there is clean, I can work with it.

'Maybe,' I teased.

'Maybe?' Well how can we turn that into a "definitely"?'

I cut to the chase and asked her, 'Do you shave?'

'Purr-fectly clean pussy,' she said.

I'd heard that before and I had then paid the money and gone with her. She had sucked my cock - pretty well to be fair - until I stopped her and told her that I had wanted to fuck her. She offered bareback for an extra tenner, which I refused. She put a condom on me and then bent over, pulling her PVC panties to the side. Not happy with "half a view", I pulled them down entirely and that was when I realised she had been lying. I hate a hairy cunt. I don't know why; I just find it unattractive to look at. Still - the bitch had lied to get me there and get me started so, she knew I wasn't going to back out then. Although - I smiled at the memory - she probably wished she had with the way her arse had bled when I fucked that hard instead.

'Show me,' I told this lady.

'Show you my pussy?' The woman laughed. She stepped back from the car and hitched her short skirt up. She was bare underneath. 'Happy?' She was bald, as promised. There was a little rash there from where she'd only recently shaved but, that didn't bother me. I'd sooner a few spots than a jungle to deal with. 'Looks nice?' she asked.

'Sure.'

'Should feel it,' she said as she rubbed herself and slipped a finger up her cunt. I could only hazard a guess as to how much lubricant she'd applied up there for her finger to slip in so easily. I wondered if her arse was as fully lubed.

'Turn around,' I told her.

She giggled and turned around so that I could see her arse. There was a little cellulite there and what looked like a couple of insect bites but other than that, it was fairly decent. One lady once had acne over her arse which I found off putting. As I had looked down, watching my cock slide in and out of her cunt - a view I usually enjoy - I had been worried whether any of the spots were going to pop their puss on to me. Thankfully they hadn't.

The whore turned back to me and asked, 'So you want to party?'

'How much?'

'For fifty, you can have it all.'

'Only got forty,' I said. Apparently, my brain didn't care how horny I was feeling and still wanted to have itself a deal.

The whore shrugged. 'Close enough.'

I smiled. 'Get in.'

'No, no, baby… My place is just up there…' She pointed across from where I was pulled over. There was an alleyway there. 'Nice and quiet,' she said, 'we won't be disturbed.'

The place I usually fucked was about a five-minute drive from here. If she knew a closer spot where we wouldn't be disturbed, then that worked for me.

'Okay,' I said. I put the window up and turned my car's engine off before I jumped out. Already semi-hard at the thought of fucking her, I slammed the car door shut and said, 'Lead the way.'

# 17

She took my hand and led me towards the alleyway. The closer we got, the harder my dick stood. It didn't help that I was staring at her arse, the whole way, and imagining myself balls deep in her.

'So, what do you want to do?' she asked me as we entered the alleyway.

'I want you to suck me for a bit and then I want to fuck you up against the wall.'

She giggled. 'Sounds like fun to me,' she said.

When we walked a little away from the entrance of the alleyway, I said, 'This is probably far enough.' I looked back over my shoulder and couldn't see the other women so, to me, we were in the clear.

'Not yet,' she said. 'I have a good spot just up here, around the corner.'

Who was I to argue? She's the one who knows the area better than me. I continued to follow her lead. With each step I was getting more turned on at the thought of being inside of her. I just hope her cunt is tight. Nothing worse than trying to throw a penny down a tunnel.

'Round here,' she said as we neared a corner. I glanced back and could barely see any of the road from here. She was right, she *did* know a better place. Not only was it hard for us to be seen here but, we probably wouldn't be heard either, if either one of us got too loud. As she disappeared around the corner, I noticed the mess on the ground. She'd either been a busy lady or, the other ladies liked this spot too. Rubbers, used, everywhere.

'Should we hang a sock out or something? So other people know the alleyway is in use?' I stepped around the corner and froze. There was a group of men standing there with one of them standing a few feet in front of the others. It was him who was grinning from ear to ear as the hooker walked up to his side and put her arm around him.

Confused, I asked, 'What's this?' It was a rhetorical question. I knew what this was. A fucking ambush.

The man at the front looked me dead in the eye and said, 'This is my bitch.' Before I could say anything, he punched me square in the face. I fell back, tripping over my own two feet, and landed on my arse. 'What the fuck you think you going to do with her?' I didn't get up. The man walked over and loomed over me. His friends joined him as the woman - the cunt - took a step back. 'You think you going to fuck my woman?' He turned to the woman and asked, 'Is that what happened here? How much he offer?'

'Forty.'

'Forty? Well shit.' He turned back to me. 'That all you think my bitch is worth?'

I opened my mouth and instantly tasted the strong flavour of iron on my tongue. I retched. They laughed. The man was the first to stop laughing. The smile faded from his face. Then, he punched me again. As stars blurred my vision, he patted me down until his hand pressed against my wallet. He pulled it open and opened it up.

'You paying her forty but have fifty in here,' he said as he took the money out. 'Well… you *had* fifty.' He laughed as he pocketed the money. Then, with a grin on his face, he said, 'You were going fuck her for forty. Well now we're going to fuck you for fifty.'

I rolled onto my front and started to crawl away, dribbling blood the whole way. I could hear them behind me, closing in. I knew it wasn't over.

'Where the fuck you think you're going?'

# 18

Winded as a heavy boot slammed into my gut. I flipped onto my side and curled into a ball as I gasped for air. Pain as another boot from someone else hit my spine with a loud, unpleasant crack. I cried out. They laughed. Another kick to my spine and I rolled onto my back due to both force and pain of the kick. I begged for them to stop. They laughed. A hand grabbed my suit lapel and lifted me from the concrete. Another hand slammed into my eye socket, blinding me in an instant. The same hand cracked my nose open. The same hand did the same to my cheek bone. The same hand split my top lip and splintered a tooth. Pain. The other hand released my jacket and I fell back to the concrete, hitting the back of my head in the process. A foot in my ribs. I rolled onto my side. A boot in my back. I rolled onto my back. A hand grabbed my ankle. Another hand grabbed my other ankle. My legs were parted.

'Do it, baby.'

A cackle.

A high heeled shoe crushed down between my legs. I screamed as everything around me continued getting darker and darker. The shoe lifted away from my bollocks. Warmth spread through my groin. Piss or blood? Another boot stamped down into my gut. I gasped for oxygen through the pain.

'See if he has a mobile.'

Hands patted me down all over once again. Car keys taken. Mobile phone taken.

'What's this?'

Hand in my pocket.

'Why the fuck have you got a dice in your pocket? What? You a gambling man?'

Couldn't answer, even if I wanted to. Barely conscious.

'I've got a game we can play. You feeling lucky?'

I coughed blood.

'I'm going to roll this here die. If it lands on, say, one to three… I'm going to let you live. If it lands on anything else… You're not going to leave this alleyway in anything but a bodybag.' There was a pause. 'How does that sound?'

I couldn't answer. I was still gasping for air and struggling to stay conscious.

I heard the dice drop to the ground. It bounced a couple of times before it came to a standstill. I couldn't see its face. With effort and through the pain, I wheezed, 'What does it say?' I said it louder, 'What does it say?' Again, 'What does it say?!'

**END**

**A note from the author:**

Either play again or go to the back of the book for a guide to which chapters run together, to give you another reading experience. Obviously, I suggest you play again but, each to their own!

# 19

I parked on my drive and turned the engine off. I glanced over to the passenger side where she was sitting and - just to be sure - I asked her, 'You really want to come in?'

'I wouldn't have had you drive me back here if I didn't,' she said.

'I know. I was just making sure. And just so you know, before you come in, when you want to go home just give me a nudge and I'll take you, okay?'

She laughed.

'What's funny?' I asked.

'You're talking to me like I should be feeling nervous, or something, but you seem more nervous than me.'

I felt my face flush. 'I do?'

She nodded.

'I'm sorry.'

'Don't be,' she said, 'it's cute.'

I'm sure my face burned brighter. *Cute*? That was the first time someone had called me "cute". I didn't know whether it was a compliment or an insult but then, if it was a bad thing she probably wouldn't be sitting outside my house.

'So, you going to give me the guided tour?' she asked.

'Of course.' I opened my car door and paused a moment. 'Oh - just one thing…'

'Don't tell me… You have a wife and she's sleeping upstairs so we have to be quiet?'

I frowned. 'No. Not what I was going to say. I was just going to warn you I have a dog in there.'

'Oh really? You didn't say anything. What breed?'

'She's a Frenchie.'

'Cute.'

There was that word again.

'You like dogs?'

'I wouldn't have one because I'm always at work but, yes, I like them. Well, some of them. Some dogs can be quite aggressive… Or just the look of them makes me feel nervous.'

'Well - she certainly isn't aggressive. She's a licker,' I told her.

'What's her name?'

'Linds.'

'Linds?'

I nodded. 'The rescue centre named her, not me.'

'Well - are you going to introduce us?'

I smiled; happy that she wasn't put off by the fact I had a dog. 'Sure,' I said.

I climbed from the car. She got out on her side and, we both closed the doors. I started towards the front door to unlock it to save her waiting around now that it had started to drizzle. By the time she caught up with me, I had opened the door.

'After you,' I said.

'I won't get attacked by Linds, will I? She won't think I'm breaking in?'

I laughed. 'She'd be a shit guard dog but, no, she's locked in her room.'

'She has a whole room?'

'Well, yes. Easier to keep track of any accidents if I am out and about.'

'I see. Not toilet trained.'

'No. She's trained. Just better to be safe than sorry.'

'Sensible,' she said as she stepped in.

I stepped in behind her and closed the front door behind us. She was standing in the hallway, looking around. Unsure of where she lived and what her home was like, I made an excuse, 'It's not much but it's mine.'

'It's nice,' she said.

I knew she was just being nice. It wasn't horrible and I wasn't embarrassed to bring someone back; I always kept it clean and always used plug-in air fresheners due to being paranoid about the dog smell. It was fairly small with one bedroom upstairs, along with a small office. There was a bathroom and the previous owners had put an ensuite in the bedroom, which I found to be weird but didn't mind. Downstairs had a kitchen, living room and a closet under the stairs and that was pretty much it. There was space for one car to park. Really, it was a perfect little "single person's" home. Any bigger would have been wasted on me.

She asked, 'Do I get the guided tour?'

I laughed. 'Not much to see. But you do get to meet Linds.'

'Ah yes. Where is she?'

Whenever I went out, I locked Linds in the living room. She had a bed in there (although she preferred to sleep on the settee), she had her toys and, because I spoil her, I always leave the television on low volume for her so that she could sit and watch it, something she did frequently.

'She's through there,' I said as I pointed to the living room. 'Ready to get licked to death?'

'From you or the dog?'

Not for the first time, I blushed again as she laughed. I like her humour and the lines she comes out with but, at the same time, I'm not used to it. Or rather, I'm not used to hearing it aimed at me.

She added, 'I'm just teasing.'

I quickly responded, 'Well that's a shame.'

Now it was her turn to blush. I walked over to the living room door and put my hand on the handle. I could already hear Linds on the other side of the door, frantic to see who I had brought home. Hopefully she'd play nice and not be jealous. Until I'd met Linds, I've never known a dog to be so obvious when they were feeling jealous about something.

I turned back to my date and asked, 'Ready?'

# 20

It was a little after midnight and we were snuggled up together on the sofa. Linds was in her bed, on the other side of the room. Whenever my date and I laughed, Linds would cast a jealous eye over in our direction. Even though it had been so long since I had been out with anyone, or even had anyone to the house, Linds wasn't happy for me. There was a part of me which was sad because of how she clearly felt; like I wasn't allowed to live a life. When I'm next alone, I'll take the time to reassure her that she is my number one but, until then, I wasn't going to push a potential partner away because of how the dog was feeling. I was just going to live in the moment and enjoy myself. Worry about tomorrow when tomorrow finally comes.

'So what number date am I?' Her question came out of the blue and took me by surprise.

'What do you mean?' I asked her.

'I mean how many dates have you had, from that site, before me?'

'You are my first,' I told her. It wasn't a lie. I'm not the sort of person that likes to talk to lots of people at once. I like to get to know someone and see where it goes first. It's hard to learn about someone when there are multiple people in the picture. At least, I find it hard. From office talk I hear, other guys don't tend to have the same problem but that's them. I'm not like them.

'First girl that agreed, huh?'

'First and only girl I have spoken to,' I clarified.

'Really?'

The way she spoke suggested I wasn't her first date, or the only person she had spoken too. I decide against asking her about her history. Again, it's not something I need to know. We all have a past life and sometimes it is better if we don't know. For instance, she doesn't need to know about my ex-wife. Or rather, she doesn't need to know about what happened between us.

'I liked talking to you,' I told her.

'But what if you met me and hated me?'

'Well, I was fairly confident that wouldn't happen but, if it had, then I would go back to the site and try again. I'm not interested in talking to loads of different people at once. I want to get to know who I am talking to, and it gets muddled if you're talking to a number of people.'

'Unless you keep a notebook.'

'A notebook?'

She laughed. 'You know, you write their name and a list of things they like and don't like. Then when you go on a date with them, you can flip to their page and jog your memory.'

I didn't know what to say but I think it's fair to say I've just found out for sure that I'm not the only person she is talking to.

She laughed again and said, 'I'm teasing. You're the first person I've met from the site.'

'Really?'

She nodded.

I told her, 'I would have thought you'd have had loads of guys hitting on you.'

'Well, I mean, I've had loads of guy's sending me pictures of their dicks.'

'That really is a thing?'

'Unfortunately.'

'One guy - Tim Miller - sent me a video.'

'A video?'

'Just cranking one off.'

'Gross.'

'Needless to say, he was blocked.'

'What kind of man does that?'

'A sad one. It wasn't even an impressive dick. It was like he was slapping a baby prawn between his fingers. Surprised I couldn't hear it screaming.'

'Well, I don't even know the guy but there's a lovely mental image.' I asked, 'I'm really the first person you've met from the site?'

She nodded. 'I liked you. I wanted to see where it went.'

I smiled and a surge of adrenaline went through me as I imagined kissing her. In fact… I reached down into my pocket and took the dice out. She frowned. 'What's that for?'

I smiled at her again and - without saying - I rolled the dice onto the glass coffee table. It stopped in the centre. She looked at me and asked, 'Should I be scared?'

## ROLL THE DICE!

**1-3:** *Make a move*
**Go to Chapter 25**

**4-6:** *Loss of control*
**Go to Chapter 21**

# 21

'I was going to kiss you,' I told her.

'Was?' She looked at the dice. 'Numbers not on my side?' I shook my head. I'm not entirely sure but, she might have looked a little disappointed. 'Well,' she said, 'I hope one day you won't need to roll the dice if you want to kiss me. You'll just be able to do it.'

I didn't know what to say so just smiled. I hope that would be the case one day too but, I've rolled the dice for all major decisions for so long now that I'm not sure if I'll ever be free from it now. A concern that, if I go against the numbers, I'll be plagued with bad luck and punished by whatever controls the dice roll. I don't know. It makes sense to me, even if no one else would understand.

Suddenly she leaned close to me and kissed me on the lips. It was a gentle kiss, her lips slightly parted. She pulled away by a fraction and said, 'You didn't kiss me. I kissed you so it's not cheating.'

I couldn't help but to grin like - I'm sure - an idiot. She smiled too and leaned into me for a second time. Once again, she instigated the kiss but, this time I responded. As she said herself, it wasn't cheating. She pulled away, leaving me wanting more. She downed the last of her drink and said, 'I think you should get me another drink and then I think you should show me upstairs.' There was a spark in her eyes and a wicked grin on her face. I couldn't help but smile. Maybe she was my ticket to living a life without the dice. Well, at least for *some* of my decisions.

'Another wine?'

'Would be great,' she said.

I quickly got up and hurried through to the kitchen where the bottle of white was waiting in the fridge. It's funny, I've heard stories about people going on date after date on these websites and never finding their perfect partner. The more time I spend with her, the more I think I've found mine and, on the first date no less. I tried to rein my thoughts in a little as I didn't want to get too carried away just yet. It was, after all, our first date and for all I know, she has some disgusting habits that she's currently hiding from me.

I took the wine from the fridge and poured her another glass. I didn't put the wine back in the fridge. Instead, I took both her glass and the bottle back to the living room where she was waiting. She saw the bottle in my hand and laughed.

'Trying to get me drunk?'

'Not at all. But if you want another glass, the bottle is there,' I told her. I passed her glass to her and set the bottle down on the coffee table. In turn, she passed my glass to me.

'Here's to a great night,' she said.

'To a fantastic night,' I said. Our classes clinked together and we both drank as, from the corner of the room, Linds barked at us out of jealousy. I finished my wine and turned to the dog, 'No!' Linds responded by lying back down on her bed. She made a little whining noise. 'I'm sorry,' I said, 'I guess she isn't used to sharing me.'

'I don't think she likes me.'

'I don't think she'll like anyone who tries to take her daddy away from her.'

She laughed. 'Then she'll hate me.' She looked me dead in the eye and - still with that wicked glint in her eyes - she asked, 'You going to take me upstairs then?'

Unable to help myself, I looked over to the dice.

She quickly changed her question to a statement before I had the chance to roll, 'Take me upstairs!'

Who was I to argue? I leaned over to the table and grabbed the wine before I stood up. I frowned.

'You okay?' she asked.

'I...' I didn't know. My legs felt wobbly. The room was spinning. I tried to say something, but the words stuck in my throat and only a strange garbled noise came out, as spots started flashing in my vision.

'You might want to sit down before you...'

## **BLACKNESS**

# 22

Her voice: 'Wakey, wakey…'

I opened my eyes. My vision blurred into focus. I could hear Linds barking from - I think - the kitchen. From her barking, she sounds like she is trapped somewhere.

I was still in the living room. Still on the floor. The only difference was, I was tied up with cable-ties. I couldn't hide my confusion. She laughed.

'How's the head?' she asked.

My head was throbbing, right across the forehead. I felt as though I had been smacked with a cricket bat, or something equally solid.

'What's going on?' I asked. Was this just a sick joke? Was she playing around? If she was, I didn't find this very funny. 'Can you undo these?' I asked as I struggled against the cable ties.

She was sitting on the edge of the sofa, looking at me. With a serious face, she told me, 'I'm afraid I lied to you.'

'What are you talking about?'

'You're not the first person I've met from the site.' She continued, 'You won't be the last either.' She smiled as she held up one of my own kitchen knives.

'What the fuck is this?'

'That's not the only lie either.' She said, 'I'm afraid to tell you, I don't like dogs either. Any size. They're all mutts.'

I tried to look towards the kitchen door but it wasn't easy from this angle. I asked, 'Where's Linds?'

'She's in the kitchen.'

'Why is she barking like that? What have you done to her?'

She giggled. 'Did you know she could fit in the microwave?'

'What?!'

'I wasn't sure to start off with. It was definitely a squeeze.'

'Bullshit. You're lying.'

She looked at me with a confused expression. She asked, 'Why would I lie?'

I didn't know what to say. 'Please don't hurt her,' I said.

'Are you begging?' she asked. She giggled again. 'I like that. Beg.'

With no other option, but still struggling, I begged, 'Please don't hurt her… Please…'

'You sound pathetic. You all do when you beg. You all sound the same.'

'Why are you doing this?'

'Because it's what men deserve.'

'What are you talking about? I've done nothing to you. I've been respectful…'

'Respectful? You're trying to fuck me on a first date. How is that respectful?'

'I thought it was a mutual thing!'

'You honestly believed I'd want you inside me?' She laughed. 'I don't want anyone inside me… Spreading your poison…'

'Then why go on a date?! Why talk to me for so long?'

'Because I am doing a favour to all the other women out there. I'm taking as many of you off the market as possible before you can go out and hurt them…'

'You're insane. You're *fucking* insane…'

'A little bit,' she said with another giggle. 'Anyway,' she said, 'that's enough of that. This isn't one of those films where the villain tells their entire plan to someone they think is cornered, only to then have the tables turned on them.' The smile faded from her face. She held the knife up so I could get a good look at it and she warned me, 'You're going to die today.' She paused a moment. 'But will it *just* be you?'

'Please don't do this,' I said, even though I knew I wouldn't be able to change her mind.

'Ssh,' she said as she raised a finger to her pursed lips. 'There's something I need to do before we go any further.' She reached over to the coffee table and picked up the dice.

'What are you…'

She cut me off again, 'Ssh…' Then, she rolled the dice as she asked, 'How will this story end?'

## ROLL THE DICE!

**1-3:** *Ending One*

**Go to Chapter 23**

**4-6:** *Ending Two*

**Go to Chapter 24**

# 23

She laughed. 'Oh, would you look at that... It doesn't look like the numbers are on your side tonight.'

'It doesn't work like that,' I told her in a desperate attempt to stop her from doing whatever was on her mind. 'You can't just roll the dice and act upon the number if you don't first say - out loud - what the options are.'

She shook her head. 'Those are your rules. If you hadn't guessed by now, we're playing by my rules.' She stood up.

'What are you doing?'

'You're a bit too heavy for me to drag with me to show you,' she said. 'But if it makes you feel better, you'll be able to hear what I am going to do.' She smiled at me and then blew me a kiss before she turned and hurried into the kitchen.

I called after her, 'Whatever you're doing, please don't!'

'Too late,' she said.

I screamed as, from the kitchen, I heard the "beep-beep" noises of buttons being pressed on the microwave. Linds continued to bark.

'Please don't…. Please! Whatever you want, I'll do it. Anything! Please don't do this…'

From the kitchen I could hear her laughing still.

'You should see her face. She looks so sad in the eyes,' she said as Linds' barking became more and more frantic.

'Please…' I started to cry.

'How do we get this thing to work?' she called out.

'Please…'

'Ah I see. Stupid me. I just have to press the button which says "START". Obvious really but, you know, I have had quite a lot of wine…'

I screamed, 'DON'T DO THIS.'

'Oops,' she said.

I heard another "beep" from the microwave and screamed out loud as the machine hummed into life. For just a couple of seconds, Linds' barking changed pitch and then - with the sound of something popping - she fell silent. I screamed again as the microwave continued to spin. The machine stopped when I heard her open its door. The sound of something wet and sloppy slipped from within and splattered on the tiled kitchen floor.

'That is fucking disgusting,' she said, despite still laughing about it. I didn't want to think about it. I just wanted the ground to open up and swallow me down. 'You should see this,' she said. 'It really is fucking gross.' She walked back into the room, still carrying my kitchen knife with her. 'I'm sorry to report back,' she said, 'that your dog is dead but, if it makes you feel any better… You're next.'

'Fuck you,' I hissed.

She sat back down on the settee.

# 24

'Actually, you can roll this,' she said. She grabbed the dice from the table again and tossed it down onto my chest. 'Just roll onto your side and we'll count that as a roll.'

'What am I rolling for?' I asked.

'Whether you scream when you die or stay as silent as possible.'

'Fuck you.'

She laughed.

I have a question for you…'

And I wouldn't answer it.

'Are you happy?'

What the fuck was she talking about.

'Your life - up to now... Was it a good one? Are you happy with it? Or rather, were you happy with it?'

I wouldn't answer.

'What's this? The silent treatment? Isn't that what us women are supposed to do?' She laughed. 'Come on, be honest, were you happy with your life up until now?'

'Does it change anything?' I asked.

'No. I just want to know whether you're going to miss "life" or whether you think I'm doing you a favour.'

I laughed. If only she knew. I'm lonely. I'm picked on at work. I hardly have any money in the bank. I'm not happy with life, no. But that didn't mean I was ready to die either. Instead of giving her an answer either way, I told her, 'Just fucking do it already. Or are you all mouth? Maybe you're getting cold feet?'

'Do you know how many people I've taken off that website now?' she asked. 'How many women I've saved from men like you...'

'I've done nothing wrong.'

'And you think I'm getting cold feet? Maybe I'm just enjoying myself? Maybe I'm just taking my time?' She said, 'Maybe I'm waiting for you to roll over to make the dice roll... See if you die screaming or die quiet...'

'Go fuck yourself.'

She smiled. 'After I'm done with you, maybe I will? I can't deny that this gets me nice and wet...' Her smile turned to laughter. I spat at her and my frothy spittle hit her square on the cheek. She stopped laughing and shook her head in disappointment as she wiped away my mess. Now I was the one smiling.

She dropped to her knees and - without a word - pressed the knife against my throat. She slit to the right.

Pain.

Hot blood.

Increased heartbeat.

Her laughing.

A spray of red.

Vision blurred.

Numb body and...

**END**

**A note from the author:**

**Either play again or go to the back of the book for a guide to which chapters run together, to give you another reading experience. Obviously, I suggest you play again but, each to their own!**

# 25

I couldn't help but smile at her. 'Should you be scared?' I said, repeating what she had asked. 'I mean I hope not.'

'So, are you going to tell me what you rolled for?' she asked.

'No.' I shook my head. 'I'm going to show you.' With the roll of the dice on my side, I leaned forward and raised a gentle hand to the side of her head as I leaned in for a kiss. She didn't pull back, much to my relief, but then - I was fairly confident she wasn't going to.

After a few more seconds, locked together in bliss, I pulled away from her. She was grinning as much as I was.

'That was unexpected,' she said.

'In a good way I hope.'

She giggled. 'Maybe.' She looked over her shoulder and towards the door.

'What's wrong?' I asked. 'Looking to run away now?'

She turned back to me, still smiling, and said, 'Not at all… Remember when you let me choose your food at the restaurant?'

I frowned, unsure as to where this going.

'Yes?'

'Well, I think you should show me around your house.'

'You want the guided tour?'

She giggled again. She had such a cute little laugh. Whenever I heard it, I couldn't help but smile and - as weird as it might sound - I wanted it as an alert on my phone. 'I do. But I want you to show me the bedroom first,' she continued with a naughty little twinkle in her eyes. 'And because I'm telling you to show me,' she said, 'you don't have to roll the dice, do you?'

'Definitely not,' I said. 'It's not a choice.'

'Perfect.'

She stood up and extended her hand down towards me. I took it and she helped pull me to my feet, not that I really needed any help. It was still cute though and any excuse to touch her was good for me.

'Lead the way then,' she said.

As I walked towards the door, I turned back to Linds. She was staring at us with a cocked head. As we stepped from the living room, Linds let out a little whine. Guess I'll be going to the pet store tomorrow to buy her a few treats so she remembers I love her…

---

We fell into the bedroom kissing and - with blind luck - landed on the bed where we continued to make out. I was on top of her one minute, grinding against her as we kissed. Then, the next minute, we rolled again, and she was on top of me. She sat up and rocked back and forwards on my crotch as she looked down at me. She grinned. 'A little excited, are we?' she asked as I poked her through my suit trousers.

'Maybe a little bit,' I admitted with a sigh as she pushed more weight down onto my hard-on.

'Anything I can do to help?' she teased.

I grabbed her and rolled her over onto her back. I kissed her again as she started to fumble with my belt. The moment it was undone, she put it her hand down the front of my shorts and took me in hand. I stopped kissing her long enough to gasp. We started kissing again.

She begged, 'Fuck me.'

Who was I to argue? I reached for one of my spare dice on the bedside cabinet and rolled it.

'What the hell are you doing?' she asked, clearly surprised by the fact I'd stopped to roll the dice. I didn't have a choice though. I couldn't continue with my night without the roll as it would have been bad luck. 'I'm telling you to fuck me,' she said. 'You didn't need to roll the dice!' With frustration in her voice, she continued, 'Please tell me the numbers are on our side…'

I laughed as I cast an eye back to the dice.

## ROLL THE DICE!

**1:** *A New Me*
**Go to Chapter 26**

**2-6:** *The Old Me*
**Go to Chapter 27**

# 26

We were lying in bed together, naked. Our clothes were in a heap on the floor where we'd ripped them off each other. I was lying on my bed, and she was cuddled in with her hand on my chest.

'Your heart is still racing,' she said.

I laughed. 'I guess I'm not too fit anymore.'

'Oh I don't know about that. You seem pretty fit to me,' she said with a little giggle.

'I'm glad you recognised the extra effort I was putting in,' I jokingly told her. In response she kissed me on my chest and cuddled in closer still.

'Thank you for a lovely evening,' she said. 'I can't tell you how refreshing it is to meet someone who actually seems genuine.'

'Guessing you've kissed a lot of frogs to find your prince then?' I asked. I'm not sure why I asked though, given I didn't want to know about people she'd seen before me. Again, that was her past. You can't change the past and it's unhealthy to fixate upon it. Live in the present and work for your future. Leave the past there.

'Thankfully I didn't have to kiss too many,' she said. I can't deny I was relieved to hear this. She continued, 'Although, are you actually a prince? Got a nice big castle somewhere and this is just your weekday digs?'

'Ha. I wish.' If I was a prince, I wouldn't have to go back to the office, although we had both decided already that we'd be calling in sick in the morning. In the morning? In a few hours. It was a little after three in the morning and, on a normal day, both of our alarms would be sounding off in in less than four hours. Neither of us relished the idea of going to work with such little sleep. I just wished I could stay off work for the rest of my working life though. At least, off from working in that office. I would be more than happy to earn my money working in someplace where I wasn't surrounded by arseholes.

'What are you thinking? she asked.

Without a thought, I replied, 'Work.'

'Oh that's great,' she said as she laughed. 'I'm that interesting, huh?'

'No, no, it's nothing to do with you. Well, it is… It's just, I've had a great night. You make me feel something I haven't felt in as long as I can remember and the thought of leaving you to go to work is… Well, it's crap.'

'I thought we were calling in?'

'But I have to go back at some point.'

'What's wrong with it?'

Normally I would just say "nothing" and leave the conversation there but, with her, I felt as though I could tell her everything and she wouldn't judge me or mock me. I felt like she was a "safe space" for my thoughts and emotions. I'd not ever felt that before; not truly. Not even with my ex. I told her, 'I'm the runt of the office.'

She laughed. 'What?!'

Whilst her laugh distracted me a moment, as I didn't find what I'd said funny, I explained, 'From day one they've never liked me.'

'Clearly they have no taste then.'

'They've always kind of been dicks to me, to be honest. Sometimes it is like being in a playground with a bunch of school kids. Or a zoo…'

'I'm sorry.'

'It's fine. Just, when I have a nice time like this evening… Makes it harder to go back to the office, you know?'

'I get it. I can't face dealing with brattish kids tomorrow… Or is it later today?'

I glanced at the clock on the bedside cabinet to confirm the time and said, 'It's definitely today.'

'Thank God we're calling in,' she said.

'Definitely.' Being sensible we had left the decision to the dice. If I had rolled a one, two or a three then we would have gone to work. Anything else and we would both call in sick and go and get some breakfast together. I told her I wouldn't have to roll the dice if she made the decision for us but, she couldn't. She wanted to take the day off with me but at the same time she felt guilty for doing so as she knew she'd be letting her colleagues down. She agreed that, if the dice landed on the four, five or six then it was meant to be, and she would do as they suggested.

I think we were both relieved when the number came up.

'Why don't you quit?' she asked.

I laughed. 'Whenever I went to do that, the dice went against me,' I said. 'I've actually lost count the number of times I've rolled to quit my job!'

'Well, what if I tell you to quit?'

I hesitated. 'I mean it's not cheating.'

'It's not.'

'And I've got some savings that would tide me over until I found something else.'

'Perfect.'

'Are you telling me to quit?'

She pulled away and looked me dead in the eyes. She said, 'I am telling you to quit.'

I laughed.

She leaned back against me and pressed her hand back against my chest as her little make-shift pillow. She said, 'Your heart is still beating so fast.'

I smiled. It was but not because I was out of breath and not because I was worried about the prospect of quitting my job and finding something else. My heart was beating fast because of her. Because I believed I had found the woman of my dreams and because of how happy she made me feel and how safe and secure and comfortable…

'I'm okay,' I said. I leaned down and kissed her forehead.

I was more than okay. I was *happy*.

**END**

**A note from the author:**

**Either play again or go to the back of the book for a guide to which chapters run together, to give you another reading experience. Obviously, I suggest you play again but, each to their own!**

# 27

I had told her, 'The dice say I have to fuck you multiple positions and make it last.' She almost seemed relieved having previously been worried that I was about to say I couldn't fuck her due to the roll of the dice. Well, no need to worry. We were definitely going to have sex this evening, that was never the issue. The only issue was the confusion I had felt in my brain as to how I really felt about her. I liked her, sure, but - I couldn't deny who, or what, I really was.

---

Clothes on the floor, scattered from where we had stripped each other, tossing the garments over our shoulders.

She was on top. Riding me. Back arched, head back, moaning as she enjoyed every inch. She feels so tight. Wet.

My hands on her arse cheeks, squeezing them. My eyes on her breasts and erect nipples. I sat up and gave them - each in turn - a little flick of my tongue. She sighed as I did so.

I rolled her onto her back. She wrapped her legs around me as I started driving into her in missionary. Her eyes closed as she bit her bottom lip. She turned her head to the side exposing her neck. I kissed it first and then gently nibbled. Her legs squeezed me tighter as her nails dragged down my back, digging in - to the point of almost being painful. I grabbed her wrists and pinned her hands back, either side of her head. She opened her eyes and looked at me with a wicked smile on her face. I started to fuck her harder. She kept her eyes locked on mine.

---

Her voice was muffled. Her face buried into the pillow. Her hands gripped the sheets and scrunched them up. On her knees with her arse up. I was behind her, fucking her deep and unable to take my eyes off her inviting little arsehole. A lick of my thumb and I started circling it, tickling and teasing her. I wanted to cum but, at the same time, I didn't want this to end. From her noises, she was enjoying it too and was getting louder with each of my thrusts.

Suddenly her whole body shuddered. I felt her pussy clamp around my erection, squeezing it hard. As her orgasm rippled through her, I thrust as deep as I could and - hands on her hips - pulled her back onto me. I held her there for a moment. She turned her head to the side and took in a lungful of air as she gasped. Her face was flushed red. When I felt her orgasm was completely finished, I pulled out.

'Mmmmm,' escaped her lips.

But I wasn't done yet.

Still with my hands on her hips, I re-positioned myself and buried my face between her legs where I started to gently kiss her sensitive pussy.

'Oh fuck,' she moaned as she pushed back into my face, allowed me to kiss her deeper. A few more kisses, varying with technique.

I pulled away.

She rolled onto her back and parted her legs for me to get easier access, the whole time with *that* wicked grin on her face.

I kissed my way up her leg, stopping at her inner thigh to give it a gentle, teasing bite. Then, I moved past her waiting pussy and gave it a little blow of warm breath. She pushed down into the mattress as I did so and then gasped as I nibbled her other inner thigh. I looked up at her. She was looking at me with an expectant, horny look on her face. I put my mouth close to her wet pussy again and held it there.

'Kiss me,' she begged.

I grinned and, unable to contain myself any further, I started with another gentle kiss against her aching clitoris. She let out a sigh, and a second one when I kissed harder. Her legs wrapped around my back, locking me in position. Her hands, on either side of my head, pulled me deeper into her.

I resumed licking and kissing and nibbling… She sighed in pleasure as she writhed into my face. I'd stay here until I could taste another orgasm coat my tongue.

'Don't fucking stop,' she sighed.

———

I was sitting on the edge of the bed. She was on her knees, a pillow on the floor for her comfort. Her mouth was wrapped around my cock. Her tongue flicking against it as she bobbed up and down. Her hand fondling my balls and gently squeezing and pulling on them. She pulled away for a moment and looked at my face as her other hand started working my shaft, firm and fast.

'I want to taste you,' she said. She sunk her mouth back over the head of my cock and sucked on the sensitive helmet as, with her hand still working the shaft, I felt an orgasm building within my body.

Ever the gentleman, I warned her, 'I'm going to cum.'

She didn't pull away. Instead, she swallowed my entire shaft to the back of her throat. My body twitched as the orgasm hit and she squeezed both testicles in one hand as I fired my hot, sticky load straight down her throat.

Only once my cock had stopped twitching did she let it slide from her mouth. I laughed due to how sensitive it now felt. She looked me in the eye and said, 'Yummy.'

'Well, that was fucking intense,' I said as I slumped back onto the bed and took a moment to capture my breath. She climbed up onto the mattress and laid next to me, also on her back as she wiped her mouth clean with the back of her hand.

'You taste great,' she said.

I couldn't help but laugh. 'As do you.'

I got up from the bed.

'Where are you going?' she asked.

'Bathroom,' I said, with a little point of my finger towards the ensuite. 'I'll be right back.'

'For round 2?' she said with the same grin on her face.

I smiled and looked down at my flaccid cock. She'd sucked the life out of it. 'Maybe,' I said. Usually, I was a one-shot kind of guy, which is why I liked to concentrate on the women first to ensure their time was enjoyable. That being said, if anyone could make me hard again it would be her.

Not getting why I was only a "maybe", she rolled her eyes and said, 'Let me guess, it depends on the dice?'

I smiled. 'Something like that. Be right back,' I said.

I about turned and walked into the bathroom.

# 28

I closed the door to the ensuite, after turning the light on, and looked at my reflection in the bathroom mirror. The smile I had worn, for her benefit, faded from my face as I stared at my eyes and to the monster within. I could hear him, chattering away inside of me. *It had been too long,* he was saying, and had been saying for a few weeks now - right back to when I signed up to the dating site.

If I felt guilt like normal people, I might have felt sorry for her as she did seem like a genuinely nice person but, I feel nothing, so I don't. If anything, I am probably doing her a favour anyway. I'm saving her from heartache and pain, delivered with a shot to the chest by people too careless with her heart. Well, I'm saving her from heartache at least. There could still be pain, I guess, but like so many other things in my life, that isn't up to me.

It's up to the dice and so far, they were doing a good job of keeping our lives intertwined. If the dice liked her, she has had plenty of opportunity to be free from me.

The bathroom mirror was built into a medicine cabinet. I pulled it open and was immediately faced with several medicine bottles and packets. Pills and potions I was supposed to take, as instructed by the doctor, but always refused because I don't like the way they make me feel so fucking braindead.

I reached up and moved the bottles to one side. Behind them, there were several dice all lined in a row. I took just one of them out and closed the cabinet back up again. My reflection looked at me with a grin plastered firmly on its sadistic face. I could hear the monster within, *Are we going to do this then*? In short, yes. Yes, we are going to do this. My ex-wife is lonely in the garden and needs some company.

I clenched my fist into a loose ball around the dice and proceeded to shake my hand. Within my grip, the dice bounced around freely. Once I was satisfied that I had given it a good enough shake, I pulled the toilet chain with my other hand and the toilet flushed. Only then, with the sound of the dice's roll disguised, did I roll it onto the side.

On a roll of 1 or 2, I'll go in and fuck her again. Then, I'll kill her quick. Any other number and, well… I'll call into work and say I'm sick. Tell them I won't be able to go in and then take my sweet fucking time with her.

The dice came to a stand-still.

**ROLL THE DICE!**

**1-2:** *Fuck and Go*
**Go to Chapter 29**

**3-6:** *All the time in the world*
**Go to Chapter 30**

# 29

'Ready or not,' here I come, I called through the door as I pretended to wash my hands, after pretending to use the toilet. I turned the taps off and opened the bedroom door, ready to give her one final fuck before I did what the monster demanded. I stopped in my tracks as I stepped from bathroom to bedroom. The bed was empty. I called out, 'Where've you gone?'

From downstairs, I heard the front door slam.

I scanned the bedroom floor and noticed her clothes were missing. Confused, I crossed the room to the bedroom window and peered out. The moon's natural light was blocked by dense clouds hanging in the air and, as a result, I couldn't see shit out there. But, I'd heard the front door so… I knew she was out there somewhere.

I grabbed my trousers and threw them on before I hurried down the stairs and to the front door. I don't know why she'd just got up and left, unless she was just fucking using me. Hopefully she'd be outside, waiting on a cab and I would be able to talk her into coming back in. Tell the cab, when they got there, that they wouldn't be needed after all. Pay the driver and get them to leave before returning back to my date.

I pulled the front door open and stepped into the cold night air. First, I glanced down the street and then, when I didn't see her, I glanced up it. I frowned as I couldn't see her that way either, not even by squinting into the blackness.

Unsure of what the fuck just happened, I stood there in the cold, confused. Had she heard me roll the dice? Had she got sick of it and walked out over that? Surely not? Surely she would have said goodbye at least. I deserved that much, given the time we had shared this evening! Or maybe she had just been using me the whole time. She'd got what she wanted: An expensive dinner, all the drinks she wanted and fucked to an inch of her life… Had I been used? I laughed at the prospect and, with nothing else to do, I turned and stepped back into the house. *What a bitch*, I thought as I closed the front door behind me. *What a sneaky, deceitful little bitch.*

Linds barked from the living room doorway. She wasn't as sorry to see my date leave. I walked over to her and patted her on the head. 'You know why she was here,' I told her. 'It was never about anything else.'

Linds whined.

The problem was the monster within was awake. I could hear it shouting at me that I needed to kill for it again. It kept saying over and over that it had been too long.

Suddenly Linds said, 'It has been too long though, hasn't it?'

'Don't you start,' I told her. It wasn't the first time Linds had put her nose in my business like this and, again, it won't be the last time either. I asked her, 'What do you think I should do? Jump in my car and drive up and down looking for her?'

Linds said, 'It doesn't have to be her though, does it? The monster didn't specify it was her…'

I knew what Linds was referring to. She was referring to that time I found a victim down in the town's industrial estate. The workers had gone home for the evening and the streetwalkers had come out to play.

'You could have another one of them,' Linds said.

'I could, couldn't I?' There was no denying that it would be one way to shut the monster up, for a while at least. So I have a new choice to roll for then: I go and pick up a working girl or I go to bed and just forget today happened. Try again another day or, better yet, talk to her and find out why she ran. Maybe I could get her back and finish things properly, the way they were meant to end for her?

I stepped past Linds and walked into the living room where one of my dice was still resting on the coffee table. I grabbed it. One to three and I go to the industrial estate. Anything else and we forget today happened.

I turned to Linds and asked, 'Ready?'

Linds barked and, I rolled the dice.

It landed on a five. That was that then. The dice had spoken. I had to go to bed and forget today happened. It wouldn't please the monster but, if that's what the dice wanted…

'But you rolled earlier,' Linds said suddenly.

'What do you mean?'

'You rolled earlier. One more fuck and then kill her.'

'Yeah but she left.'

'You never specified who you would fuck and kill,' Linds said.

I paused a moment as I thought back to when I had rolled the dice in the bathroom. She was right. I hadn't actually said her name. I could have been talking about anyone when I rolled that dice and *that* dice had told me to fuck them and go so…

I grinned. 'I guess I'm going out for a couple of hours.'

Linds barked.

**Go to Chapter 16**

# 30

I stepped out of the bathroom and back into the bedroom and stopped dead in my tracks when I noticed she was up, out of bed, and putting her clothes on.

'You're going?'

She paused a moment and said, 'It's been a fun evening but I need to get home. I've got work in the morning and need to get home and change.' She laughed. 'I think our second date should be on a weekend, or at least at a time when we're both better prepared.' She bent down and picked her bra up off the floor and proceeded to put it on as I just stood there, watching and surprised by what she was doing. She continued, 'I should probably call in sick. I'm going to be good for nothing but, if I do that, it screws my colleagues over so… Guess the kids get an easy lesson of watching a film or something.' She laughed again as she reached for her dress. She put it over her head and wriggled down into it.

'You're leaving.'

'I'm not running out,' she said.

'I mean, that's what it feels like in all honesty.'

'I like you,' she said. 'I want to see you again.' She hitched up her dress to show her panties and - with a smile - asked, 'Did you want to keep these? Still wet… Fragrant'

Inside, I could hear the monster screaming at me to stop her. 'You can't go now,' I told her.

She pulled her dress back down and started looking around on the floor. 'Have you seen my phone?' she asked. I had but that didn't mean I was going to tell her. 'Unless you want to be a gentleman and call a cab for me?'

'I can take you home,' I told her. I *could* take her home too but, really, I was imagining driving her out somewhere quiet, raping her and then throttling her to death.

'You've been drinking,' she said. 'Pretty sure you'd still be over the limit.' Newsflash, you stupid bitch, I was probably over the limit last night too, when I drove us both back here.

'I feel fine,' I said.

'It's okay. I'm a big girl. I can get a taxi.' She added, 'I must have left my phone downstairs.' She took a step towards the bedroom door. I quickly blocked her path. 'What are you doing?'

'You're not going anywhere,' I said.

The smile on her face faded. She frowned. 'I have to go home so I can get whatever sleep I can before I go to work. Please can you step to the side?'

I shook my head.

'Okay, you're starting to scare me.'

A smile slowly spread across my face. 'That's the idea,' I told her.

'What is wrong with you?'

She tried to push past me, so I grabbed her and threw her back into the middle of the room. She tripped over her own feet and landed on the floor with a shocked expression on her face. I didn't move from the doorway. I was just standing there, savouring her new fear.

'Please let me go home,' she said.

I slowly shook my head. 'I rolled the dice.'

'What? What does that even mean? Rolled the dice for what?'

'What do you think?' I continued to smile as I let that sink in. From her expression I could see that she understood.

She said again, 'I want to go home.'

I slowly shook my head. 'Not happening.'

'I'll scream.'

'I know.'

She jumped up and ran towards me. Without hesitation, I slammed my fist into her face and sent her crashing back down onto the floor with a bloody nose and split lip. She cried out in pain. I don't know what the hell she was thinking. She's a petite girl, did she just think I was going to jump out of her way and let her leave? I laughed at her stupidity as she laid there, crying and moaning in pain.

'That was entirely your fault,' I told her. 'Now… Are you ready?' I took a step towards her. Enough chit chat. It was play-time.

# 31

I pulled her up onto the bed and laid her down flat on her back. She had fought me for a bit so I'd been forced to punch her in the face for a second time. This time my fist had connected to her eye socket which was already turning black and swollen shut. She certainly wasn't as pretty now as she had been at the start of the night.

I'd removed her clothes again and set most of them down on the floor. Her panties I had stuffed in her mouth which I'd then taped shut, using tape from the bottom drawer of the bedside cabinet. I had also taped around her arms and body so that she couldn't lash out. Her legs had to be taped in another way with tape wrapped around her ankles and then to the corners of the foot of the bed, forcing her legs to remain parted and her tidy little cunt exposed. She had tears coming from her good eye which looked at me with more fear than I had ever seen before.

'I was married before but it didn't work out. You know how that relationship ended?' I put my dice down on her bare stomach and told her, 'With a roll of the dice. If I rolled a one, I was going to divorce her. If I rolled anything above that then… Well…' I laughed as the memory flashed through my excited mind. 'Hopefully you'll like my wife because there's a chance you might end up next to her. A chance… You see the monster inside me makes a lot of my decisions from here on in so I don't need to roll the dice but, he doesn't enjoy cleaning up and leaves that to me so… With a few choices as to what to do with you, I have to roll the dice. You know how it is.'

She wasn't trying to talk through the panties, she wasn't trying to fight back. She was just lying there, staring me out and sniffling through her tears. For someone who had informed me they were going to scream, I couldn't help but feel a little disappointed at her lack of fight.

'I want you to know that I really do like you,' I told her. She had a right to know, I figured. 'I think we had a special connection…' I put my hand on her leg and traced a finger to her inner thigh and then up to her pussy. When I touched her cunt, she flinched. I didn't care as I started to gently stroke her. 'I feel, if I didn't have this *thing* inside me that we could have gone the distance too.' Her pussy was dry to the touch but it didn't stop me from forcing my finger inside her. She winced. 'I'm guessing from the way you were talking earlier that you felt the same too, which was nice to hear.' I confessed, 'I just wish I didn't have this thing in me... But I do and so... I need to do this or else I'd lose my mind.' I added, 'I hope you understand.' I pulled my finger out and gave it a sniff. I could smell more of the rubber that I'd used earlier than her actual pussy; something I often found disappointing when in this situation. I shrugged it off as my mind went back to the task at hand.

I need a knife.

I got up from the bed and walked to the door before I paused to tell her, 'I'll be back in a minute, okay? I need to get something.' Without explaining what - she would see soon enough - I hurried down the stairs and towards my kitchen.

# 32

I grabbed the biggest knife from the kitchen and admired the sharpness of the blade. Given how much I had used it in the past, I wasn't sure whether it would be any good still but, looking at it now, it would still do what was necessary. I smiled at the thought of slowly pushing the blade into her and giving the handle a little twist to ensure her insides were truly ripped. Funny how fingering her earlier had done nothing for my flaccid, exposed penis and yet the thought of piercing her with the blade gave me a semi-on. I laughed at myself. The monster was well and truly in control of my body now.

Whilst I was down here, I figured I would pop my head in on Linds and let her know that I still love her. With how "lovey-dovey" I had been being earlier with my date, there was a part of me which was worried Linds had believed it too.

I left the kitchen and walked down the hallway towards the living room. With a warm, friendly smile on my face for Linds, I peered into the room and - *Fuck.* She wasn't there. I was expecting to find her asleep in her bed but... Wait. Noises.

From upstairs I could hear my date whining through the panties. Oh God. Linds must have gone upstairs whilst I was in the kitchen. Knife in hand, I hurried up the stairs and back to the bedroom. I froze in the doorway and, a split second later, I started to laugh.

'Linds! What the fuck do you think you're doing?'

Linds was on the bed with her little tail wagging. She was greedily licking at my date's exposed cunt as she, herself, writhed around in a desperate (and futile) attempt to get free.

I walked over to the pair of them and pushed Linds away. 'I'm sorry about that,' I said, 'she doesn't usually do that to the ladies I bring back. Guess you must taste a little salty, or something.' It was hard not to chuckle. From where I pushed her down onto the floor, Linds barked. I turned to her with a stern expression on my face. Well, as much of a stern expression as I could muster under the fucked-up circumstances. 'You know you're not supposed to do that. That's daddy's favourite snack. It's not for you…' I set the knife down on the floor and glanced back to the moist pussy. It was pretty gross that Linds had been licking it but, fuck it… Pussy is pussy. I leaned forward and gave it a lick too. My "date" squirmed at my tongue. I looked up and asked, 'Be honest, who has the better technique?' I laughed at my own joke although, now I'd said it, I did wonder who the better cunt-eater was. I shook the thought from my mind as another idea popped in there.

Without a word I leaned over to the bedside cabinet and opened the top drawer. I pulled out a little tub of lubricant - Linds' favourite flavour. With a dirty grin on my face, and a stiffening cock, I scooped out a healthy dollop of the gel and smeared it into my backside. I set the lube back on the cabinet and re-positioned myself between my date's legs.

'Okay!' I said in an excited tone to Linds. Whenever I did that, in that specific tone, Linds knew she was "okay" to do whatever she was pining for. As I started to lick out the dog-flavoured pussy once more, Linds jumped back up on the bed and started tongue-fucking the gel out of my arsehole. As I worked my tongue, Linds worked hers and - it was fucking sublime. 'Oh shit,' I muttered as she got her tongue nice and deep inside me.

I moved slightly and reached down to the knife. I grabbed it by the handle and moved myself back to the saliva-drenched slit. I knew I wouldn't last long with Linds' tongue working overtime in my arse and I'd already decided how I wanted to ejaculate… *Shit*. The thought of what I wanted to do, along with eating her pussy and having Linds lick out my arse put me over the edge and the start of my climax started tingling throughout my body.

I quickly pulled my tongue out of my date and moved up the bed until we were face to face. Linds moved up too and as I stuck my cock in my date's soaked cunt, Linds put her tongue back in my arse. I let out a loud moan as the feelings of the climax continued brewing and building and… As I fired my cum into my date, I penetrated under her chin with the knife's pointed blade. I pushed up as the orgasm continued to quiver through my body. The blade pushed through into her mouth, up into the roof of her mouth, through that, behind the nose, between the eyes and into her brain. Death was almost instant.

I left the knife inside her but pulled my cock out.

'That's enough,' I said to Linds as I gently pushed her from the bed. She jumped down and sat a moment, licking her lips.

The monster, inside, was quiet.

'Happy?' I asked it.

It didn't answer, which was proof that it *was* satisfied.

I looked at my date's body. The monster is happy, now all I have to do is clean up the mess and that's that for, hopefully, a couple more months before the monster starts talking to me once more.

I looked at the mess and my heart sank. There was nothing worse than having a great orgasm and then having to clean up immediately. But then, who said I had to do it now? Maybe I could leave it? Get a little sleep first, wake up, call in sick at work and - yeah - clean up then? I guess there's the choices for my dice roll.

Okay, so one to three and I'll clean up now. Four onwards and I'll shut my eyes for a bit and then sort it. Keep it fair with a fifty-fifty chance each way.

Once again, I reached for my dice.

**ROLL THE DICE!**

**1-3:** *Clean*
**Go to Chapter 33**

**4-6:** *Rest*
**Go to Chapter 37**

# 33

I'm not happy with the dice telling me to clean the mess up before I rest but I know it's the more sensible of options. Clean up, get it all "back to normal" in here and then - when everything is sparkling - put my feet up for a well-deserved rest. It's just… I'm tired now and it would be great to just stop and have a little shut eye. That being said, I know I would be pissed to wake up and have to deal with the mess. I shook my head. It's bullshit that I have to deal with this. The monster inside me wanted this done. The monster should be the one responsible for operation clean-up.

Fuck it. I could stand here, by the bed, bitching about cleaning all fucking day and not actually get anything done. Or, I could just shut the fuck up and get it over with.

I grabbed the roll of tape I'd used earlier to tie her down and I wrapped it around her head, where the knife was still protruding. By leaving the knife in, where I stabbed her, and wrapping her head all knife and tight - it stopped excess spillage landing on the carpet and making a bigger mess. Once that was done, I put the tape down and grabbed some scissors from the bottom drawer of the bedside cabinet.

I cut the tape away from both of her ankles and tossed the scissors down on the bed as I wouldn't be needing them anymore. At least, not with her.

Next, I grabbed her by the ankle and yanked her from the bed. Her body slumped to the floor and something - not sure what exactly - cracked upon impact. Good job she was dead or else that would have really hurt.

'You know you could help one of these days,' I said to Linds. She was just sitting a few feet away, watching me intently. Lazy bitch.

I let go of her ankle and stood up straight before I stretched out my back. A little warm-up before the main event. I reached back down and grabbed her ankle again and, with much grunting and sweat, I dragged her from bedroom to ensuite.

# 34

I rolled her into the shower cubicle and folded her in as best as I could. It took a lot of willpower not to have a little more fun with her first but, the dice said I had to clean so - here I was. It was times like these in which I found myself wishing I had a bathtub but - hey ho - this would do.

Once she was in place, I leaned over to the cabinets beneath the sink. Upon opening the left-hand side, I pulled out a small electric handsaw. I used to have a bog-standard hacksaw in here but that fucking thing took an age to cut through the flesh and, well, it got old real fast. Especially as I don't actually enjoy this part of the process. The monster is fed so that side of me is quiet. The more "human" side is in charge of things and all the bone crunching and splintering noises are fairly disgusting. Usually, after ten minutes of cutting, I start feeling queasy. It's never fun and I often find myself wishing the monster would at least hang around for this part but… Well… Fuck him.

As I plugged the saw in Linds came in and started sniffing at the woman's corpse again.

'Get away from her, you idiot!' I told her. She just looked at me with her *puppy-dog* look in her eyes. 'You've already licked her half to death,' I told her. 'That's enough.'

'I don't want to lick her,' Linds said. Some people might be concerned when their dog starts talking to them, but I find it quite comforting. It shows me that, no matter how alone I often feel, I've always got Linds. Her love is unconditional. Right now, I knew what she wanted too. Once upon a time I had cut a body up, in fact it might have even been my ex-wife. There's been a few ladies stuffed into this shower now and I can't quite recall. Anyway, Linds had been licking her lips continuously as I cut away slithers of meat. There had been a hungry look in her eyes. Curious about what she was thinking, I had offered a small piece of meat before and - to my surprise - she wolfed it down with hardly a chew. I didn't give her more than that because I wasn't sure if it was going to have the same effect on her gut that chicken had. A little bit is fine but too much and she'd have soft shit for a week solid. But maybe I was being harsh? Maybe this meat would have been absolutely fine for her tummy?

I cut away a small piece of flesh and turned back to Linds. 'Ready?' I asked as she positioned herself, ready to catch it. I smiled and tossed it up in the air. She launched herself towards it and caught it in her mouth and - just as before - practically swallowed it down in one. 'Good girl!' I praised her for not dropping it and letting it splatter on the floor.

'I want more,' she said with a greedy look in her eyes.

She's a good dog. The *best*. Maybe I should save some of this for her? Maybe I could cut a load away and put it in Tupperware boxes stored in the fridge and freezer? A little treat for all that she does for me? 'Please can I have some more?'

But then, what if someone comes around here? I haven't had people sniffing around yet but it doesn't mean that they won't. What if someone knows I was the last person to see one of my victims and they come knocking with search warrants? The last thing I would want is to be caught with a load of corpse stock-piled in the kitchen.

'Come on, don't hold back,' Linds said, practically begging.

'I love you,' I told her, 'but you know I can't just decide to do this…'

'What if I *tell* you to do it?'

I shook my head. 'We need to roll the dice,' I told her.

Linds whined.

'Go and get my dice,' I told her.

Because she knew what was on the line, Linds hurried into the bedroom. She carefully picking the dice up between her teeth and came running back to me with her tail wagging from side to side. She dropped the dice on the floor.

'Okay,' I told her, 'One to three and we'll save some. Anything else and all of it goes in the garden, where the others are buried. And, just with the others, you can't go digging around there, okay?'

Linds barked. Her way of saying "yes".

'Good girl,' I told her again.

I picked the dice up and gave it a shake ahead of rolling it on the tiled bathroom floor. We both watched as the dice tumbled across the tiles.

**ROLL THE DICE!**

**1-3:** *Save some*

**Go to Chapter 35**

**4-6:** *Laid to rest*

**Go to Chapter 36**

# 35

'The dice love me!' Linds barked with enthusiasm. I smiled. It was nice to see her so happy and I'm glad the dice had sided with her.

'Probably because you have good karma,' I said as I patted her on the head. 'Remember though, we'll save some. The rest still has to go in the garden with the others and, same rules apply, you can't just go digging them up. Do we have a deal?'

'Yes! We have a deal! Thank you, thank you, thank you…' She wagged her tail from side to side probably faster than I had ever seen it wag before. I couldn't help but laugh.

'Well get back and let me sort this out,' I told her. The last thing I needed was to be cutting up the flesh only to have her stick her nose in and get sliced too. Despite her desperation for more "food", Linds backed up and watched - patiently - as I started to cut into the body.

The idea was to cut the body into smaller, manageable chunks. But all the time Linds was watching me the way she was, I couldn't concentrate properly. So, to give myself a little time, I cut away a strip of flesh and tossed it towards her. Just as before, she caught it in her mouth and swallowed it down in one.

'Go steady,' I warned her. 'Last thing I needed was for it to lodge in her throat and have to try and fish it out with my fingers.'

'One more bit and then I'll leave you to it,' she said.

'Really? Are you fucking joking me?'

She cocked her head and whined.

'Fucking hell. One more bit and then that's it for now,' I told her. I wasn't joking either. She could whine as much as she wanted but, after this, there'd be no more today. The rest would be divided between the fridge, the freezer and the shallow grave I'd already prepared out back.

'I promise… One more bit and I'll leave you in peace to finish off,' Linds said.

I shook my head and cut another strip of flesh from her. She barked with excitement. In her years on this planet, I had never seen her so excited about food before. I mean - sure - she got excited but never like this. This was a whole new level and - I can't lie - it was bordering on annoying now. I mean, how good could it be? I looked down at the meat in my hand. When it was off the body, it looked just like any other cut of white meat.

Linds licked her lips.

'It's really that good?' I asked her.

'You need to try it for yourself!' Linds encouraged me with a thought which had already crossed my mind. 'It's so fucking good,' she said.

'Is it though…?' I kept looking at the meat, wondering what it would taste like if I were to pop it in my mouth right here and now.

'Try it! You won't regret it!'

'You reckon?'

'I promise. So fucking good,' Linds said again as though she was nothing more than a broken record skipping over and over on the same line.

Quickly - before I changed my mind - I closed my eyes and tossed the lump of flesh into my mouth. I chewed it a couple of times and felt immediate repulsion as it squelched between my teeth. A squidgy, slimy lump. It was no wonder Linds just swallowed it down.

'What do you think?' Linds asked. 'It's the best, right? THE FUCKING BEST!'

'It's fucking rank,' I said as I rested the lump on my tongue, unwilling to keep chewing it. The taste, the texture… It was all just fucking grim. Just to get it over with, and still with my eyes closed up tight, I swallowed hard and…

Fuck.

It lodged in my throat.

I coughed but it didn't budge.

Panic.

Warmth spread through my entire body and I swallowed hard again in an attempt to dislodge the rancid lump. No luck. I tried to gasp for air but no air came.

'What's wrong?' Linds asked as I started flapping around as panic continued to take over my body. 'What's the problem? You're scaring me,' she said.

I swallowed again and still I couldn't budge it from my airways as my heart raced uncomfortably fast and my lungs burned hot. Still no air. Swallow hard. Still couldn't…

…budge it…

'Are you okay?' Linds asked.

I slumped forward and face planted on the floor as the room faded to black.

**END**

**A note from the author:**

**Either play again or go to the back of the book for a guide to which chapters run together, to give you another reading experience. Obviously, I suggest you play again but, each to their own!**

# 36

Linds looked at me and I was sure I could see resentment in her eyes. I'll be honest, it's not something I usually saw from her, and it wasn't particularly nice to see.

'I'm sorry, girl,' I said to her.

Without so much as a whimper, she turned away and walked back into the house as I remained in the garden with the shovel in my hand.

I know she wanted me to save her some of the meat from my date's corpse, but she couldn't always have things her way. As far as dogs go, Linds is pretty spoiled at the best of times and sometimes she just needs to learn "no". Sure, I felt shit denying her something she clearly wanted but what if I had given her the meat? What if we had saved some and scattered it in her biscuits for as long as we could keep it "fresh" for? What if, once it was gone, she started having withdrawal symptoms from it? What if she decided to come into the garden, looking for more? I'd come out and find freshly dug holes all over the place where she'd been searching for the bodies. That wouldn't do.

Sometimes you just had to say "no".

I looked down at the freshly dug earth. A few feet below, covered in lime, my date was slowly beginning to rot away. The mess was cleaned up. The monster was quiet for now and for a while, everything would go back to as "normal" as my life ever was. For how long that "normality" lasted, I do not know. Sometimes the monster within would be quiet for weeks, sometimes months and - rarely - years. I'd enjoy those quiet times, but I always find myself wondering when he was going to stick his head up again.

I cast my eyes around the rest of the garden. A stranger would see grass in need of a cut and some shrubs which needed to be pruned. I don't see that. I see bodies. So many bodies.

I sighed as I wondered how many more I would have to add to the collection before the monster left me be.

From deep inside, I heard a ripple of laugher. The monster spoke, 'How's about one more?'

'You said that last time,' I told him.

The monster laughed. 'Just one more.'

**END**

Congratulations - you found the "true" ending of the book. Want to read the other stories within her? Either play again or flip to the back of the book to see a story key which will take you to some of the other stories within!

# 37

I woke up with a start. In the dream I'd had, a creature lurking in the shadows had been chasing me all night. Every time I turned to see it, whilst running, I saw nothing but blackness. I could hear it though. This thing, hiding in the shadows and taunting me. I'd woken from my dream after it took a swipe at me. I felt its razor-sharp nails scratch down my back and - that's when I woke.

The sun was shining through the window because I'd forgotten to close the curtains when I collapsed on the bed, next to my date. Beams of light had been quietly cooking her whilst I slept, and she was starting to stink. I gagged at the stink and promptly sat up, unsure whether I was going to vomit or not.

Thankfully I didn't.

Linds was sleeping on the floor, stretched out. Usually, she liked to sleep on the bed too. I'm guessing the smell of decomposing flesh put her off. Can't lie, there was a part of me which regretted not cleaning her up before I went to sleep but - it is what it is. There's no turning back the clock, just as there's no re-rolling of the dice.

I glanced back at the corpse. Her arms were still bound to her sides, her legs still parted and taped in position. The knife still imbedded through her chin and up her face into her brain. Great tits though and I absent-mindedly found myself stroking my semi hard cock whilst staring at her breasts. I laughed when I realised what I was doing. Apparently not even the sight of a corpse, or the smell of one, can ruin my early morning horniness.

Linds whined from the floor. She was awake and staring at me.

'What do you think?' I asked her. 'Reckon it's wrong to have one last go on her before I put her away with the others?'

Linds got up and walked from the room as though she was disappointed I would even dare suggest such a thing. I swear, I love that fucking dog more than life itself, but she sure does have a jealous streak.

'I was joking,' I called out in the hope of appeasing her.

But I wasn't joking. Looking back at her body, especially her inviting little slit, and there was definitely a thought in my brain suggesting I could have one last little play-time with her before I cleaned the mess up.

My cock was hard now as the thought of lubing up and sliding into her started to play through my mind with more vivid imagery. With all I've done, not just to her but other people I've brought back here before now... Would it really be *that* wrong to have one last fuck? I mean who would know? It's only me and her in here and she sure as fuck wasn't going to tell anyone.

It dawned on me she couldn't tell me to fuck her either so, if I was going to do this, I would have to give the dice a roll and let the numbers decide. Those fucking dice. I can't remember when I first started using those, other than the fact that I had been really young. I can't remember why I became so fucking dependent on them but - what I do know - I can't go against it. I have to play the game properly or else bad things will happen.

Well hopefully the dice will be on my side today, just as they've been on my side other times too? Fingers crossed.

I reached over to the bedside table and grabbed the dice.

'Please, please, please...' I said as I mentally told myself that rolling a one to three would permit me to fuck her, and a four to six meant I'd just have to clean her up and have a wank later. If the latter did happen, there was nothing to stop me from using her panties as I did so and - with that in mind - I made a mental note to give them a good rub over her cunt before I disposed of her. Get them good and fragrant or else it's just like sniffing cotton. There isn't anything sexy about that.

With my prick twitching at the thought of being inside her, I rolled the dice and hoped for the best.

**ROLLS DICE:**

**1-3:** *One Last Fuck*
**Go to Chapter 38**

**4-6 -** *Clean*
**Go to Chapter 34**

# 38

I smiled at the dice just as - apparently - the dice smiled at me. I turned back to my date. The smile faded from my face when my eyes settled on the knife handle sticking from beneath her chin. It was hardly the most erotic of sights and - in all honesty - it kind of dampened the mood a little. I wouldn't let it kill the mood though…

One last fuck so, need to make it worthwhile. Needed to remember it given the fact she'd be buried beneath the dirt by the end of the day. I grabbed her body and rolled her onto her front so as to hide her face.

I leaned forward and pulled the pillow out from under her head. I placed it over her head to stop the possibility of accidentally seeing something I didn't want to. Just like that, the problem was sorted. I grinned again as I spat into my hand and rubbed my warm and frothy spit over my stiff prick. Good thing about the way she was lying now, it made it easier to put it in her little arsehole; something I'd yet to try out for tightness.

I climbed over her and spat into my hand for a second time. This time I rubbed my mixture into and against her arsehole. I also pushed two of my wet digits inside her to ensure some of my natural lubricant lined the walls within too, to help with my penetration. When I pulled my fingers out, I was pleased to see they were mostly clean. A little sniff test and I knew I was okay to push in, not that I would have been too bothered had she been dirty up there. A fuck is a fuck and I'd be taking a shower as soon as I'd done this and cleaned her away.

Desperate to feel her tightness, I nudged the head of my dick against her, and, with effort, I squeezed myself inside. I gasped at how tight she was as the walls of her arsehole gripped my shaft.

I held myself there for a moment, enjoying the throttling sensation. Then, I pushed in as deep as I could go before pulling mostly back out again, stopping short from slipping out entirely. I pushed in again and - soon - I was fucking her hard and deep with such force she'd surely be screaming had she been alive to tell the tale.

I started to get carried away and pounded her corpse harder and faster, grunting heavily as I did so. It felt so fucking good, being deep in her arsehole, that I couldn't slow myself even if I wanted to. And I did want to. I wanted this to last hours. I wanted to edge myself over and over again, stopping short of ejaculating. Not only would it have made for a more intense orgasm, but it would have made everything last longer too but, despite knowing this, I just couldn't bring myself to slow the fuck down.

'Fuuuck…'

I felt my blood boiling as I got closer and closer to the orgasm I so desperately wanted to delay, if only for a few more minutes of being inside her. I felt my body tingling and my heart racing and…

I stopped as a pain in my chest caused me to cry out for a different reason entirely. *What the fuck is this?* Pins and needles in my left arm as my heart skipped a beat, raced for a few, skipped another and… My face contorted as I was hit with another wave of intense pain radiating from my chest.

'Uuugghhhhhhh,' escaped my mouth. No word in particular and just a reflex as another wave of pain stabbed from the centre of my chest again. Harder this time. More painful and…

**END**

**A note from the author:**

**Either play again or go to the back of the book for a guide to which chapters run together, to give you another reading experience. Obviously, I suggest you play again but, each to their own!**

## STORY KEY

*Please be aware that the listed key is the <u>main</u> story threads only. When playing the game, you could have got the same story through a different path which could have been longer, or shorter. I didn't want to list <u>all</u> the threads (and possible routes) because I believe that takes the enjoyment from the book. To find them all, you just need to keep on rolling that dice!*

**A Roll of the Dice (main story) - EXTREME**
CHAPTERS: 1, 2, 4, 5, 12, 13, 19, 20, 25, 27, 28, 30, 31, 32, 37, 34, 36 -

**Karma (shorter version of this story, taking different routes, is in this list called "Whore")**
CHAPTERS: 1, 2, 4, 5, 12, 13, 19, 20, 25, 27, 28, 29, 16, 17, 18 -

**Happy Ever After**
CHAPTERS: 1, 2, 12, 13, 19, 20, 25, 26 -

**The Honey-Trap**

CHAPTERS: 1, 2, 12, 13, 19, 20, 21, 22, 23, 24 -

**Bullied to the end**

CHAPTERS: 1, 2, 4, 5, 6, 7, 8 -

**Victim no more**

CHAPTERS: 1, 2, 4, 5, 6, 7, 9, 10, 11 -

**A tragic life**

CHAPTERS: 1, 2, 3 -

**Whore (shortened version of "Karma")**

CHAPTERS: 1, 2, 12, 13, 14, 15, 16, 17, 18 -

Enjoyed the stories? Check out Vimeo for some of Matt Shaw's short films!

https://vimeo.com/themattshaw

Want more Matt Shaw?
Sign up for his Patreon Page!

www.patreon.com/themattshaw

Signed goodies?
Head for his store! www.mattshawpublications.co.uk

Printed in Great Britain
by Amazon